PREVIOUS CONFECTIONS

AN AMISH CUPCAKE COZY MYSTERY

RUTH HARTZLER

ROMANCE BOOKS

Previous Confections: An Amish Cupcake Cozy Mystery
(Amish Cupcake Cozy Mystery Book 2)
Ruth Hartzler
Copyright © 2019 Ruth Hartzler
All Rights Reserved
ISBN 9781922420671

Scripture quotations are from The Holy Bible, English Standard Version® (ESV®), copyright © 2001 by Crossway, a publishing ministry of Good News Publishers. Used by permission. All rights reserved.

This is a work of fiction. Any resemblance to any person, living or dead, is purely coincidental. The personal names have been invented by the author, and any likeness to the name of any person, living or dead, is purely coincidental.

I was sitting in a fancy French restaurant. I hadn't been in a restaurant since my fiftieth birthday, when my then-husband Ted had told me he was going to divorce me and marry a college student named Cherri who was expecting his baby.

I never thought I would see Ted again, much less be invited to dinner with him in a restaurant. I no longer had feelings for him, but my stomach churned at the thought of seeing him again. Ted had called unexpectedly to demand I sign papers. I had called my divorce lawyer who had advised me not to sign and had given me the name of a local lawyer here in Lancaster. The local lawyer had also told me not to sign and advised me to take the papers to him.

I looked at my watch again. Ted was five minutes late. I looked around the restaurant. Ted had assured me he wouldn't run out and leave me with the bill this time. That was just as well as I imagined the prices here were quite high. The wooden tables appeared to be of bur walnut or similar timber, and the walls were burnished copper with art installations made from copper and brass.

The lights were of unusual geometric designs, and the entire restaurant lighting was muted, no doubt in part due to the wall sconces which held real candles. I idly watched the flames playing along the walls as I snuggled into my chair. It was comfortable with a nicely padded back. Soft music settled my nerves, at least to a degree.

The entire ambience was delightful, and I wished I had been here on a date with a nice man, not waiting for my ex-husband who would no doubt turn nasty and demand I sign the papers. My mind drifted away to the person of Damon McCloud, the Scottish detective I had met recently.

I would have preferred lunch to dinner, but my twin sister Rebecca had broken her arm the previous day and had left me in charge of her Amish cupcake store.

My flatmates Eleanor and Matilda, ladies in their eighties, had offered their help, but Rebecca had suggested to me that they shouldn't help too much. I had no idea why, only that it had something to do with a previous incident that no one wanted to tell me about.

I was looking at my watch once more when I heard someone clearing their throat. My blood ran cold. It was Ted.

At Ted's shoulder was a tall, impossibly stick-thin woman who looked like a supermodel. Heavy musk perfume emanated from her in waves, and her dress was so tight I wondered how she had managed to pour herself into it.

"Jane, you're here," Ted said, stating the obvious.

"You're late," I said in the most accusatory tone I could muster.

"Well, I'm here on business of course," Ted said. "I invited you along to kill two birds with one stone, so to speak. I would like you to meet my wife, Cherri."

I stared at Cherri, my mouth open. So this is what the other woman looked like! She was less than half my age, probably closer to one-third of my age. I shook my head to clear it, when I realized Cherri was speaking.

She extended her hand. "Lovely to meet you, Jane."

I shook her hand, noticing the limp handshake. "Nice to meet you too," I lied. I mean, what was I supposed to say to the woman who had been my husband's mistress for several months while I was married to him? I supposed there was no etiquette book for that.

"Where's the baby?" I asked her.

Cherri looked surprised. "Sunshine? Oh, she's back in New York with our nanny."

I wondered if the nanny was younger and better looking than Cherri. Maybe the nanny would be my ex-husband's new conquest. If Cherri had any sense, she would have hired someone who was entirely unattractive.

Ted sat down. "Have you decided what you're eating yet, Jane?" he asked, looking at his watch and then checking his phone. He turned to Cherri and spoke in a far different tone. "And what would you like to eat, Pumpkin? Take your time."

Cherri giggled. "I already know what I'd like, Popsicle. I studied the menu online before we came.

4

I'll have the Beef Carpaccio, and for the main I'll have the Pheasant Roulade."

"What about you, Jane?" Ted snapped before looking at his watch again.

"I didn't study the menu online first," I said, casting a quick glance at the menu. "I'll have the Oyster Crudo followed by the Lemon Sole Veronique." I didn't particularly like oysters and I didn't know what the Lemon Sole Veronique was as the description was in French, but they were the most expensive things on the menu and Ted had said he was paying.

After we ordered, Ted said, "Excuse me. While we wait for our meals, I need to converse with my clients. You two can chat." With that, he left the table and hurried away.

Could this be more awkward? I was sitting with my husband's former mistress, now his wife, and I wanted the floor to open up swallow me, but Cherri did not appear awkward at all. "So Jane, have you turned Amish again?"

Was I imagining it, or was she staring at my clothes? Sure, I had made my own dress, but I thought it was quite nice, a far cry from a long plain dress, apron, prayer *kapp* and sensible shoes. I reminded myself that Cherri would not know what

Amish women wore. I shook my head. "No, I left the Amish after my *rumspringa* when I was sixteen. My twin sister and her family are Amish."

Cherri did not respond but posed another question. "Have you lived in Lancaster for long?"

"Since Ted and I separated," I said, wondering if it would embarrass her. "Why are you both here in town?"

Cherri leaned forward and addressed me in a conspiratorial manner. "Melissa and Marcus Matheson own this restaurant. They've come here from New York to check on it."

"Oh," I said, although Cherri seemed to think I should be impressed.

Cherri pushed on. "Melissa and Marcus are ever so rich, you see. They're rolling in it, if you get what I mean." She broke off and giggled. "Ted has known them for many years. Surely you know the Mathesons?"

I had to admit that I didn't.

Cherri was obviously surprised at my ignorance. "Why Jane darling, they're *ever so* rich," she said yet again. "They have a restaurant in New York as well. They've sent their top chef, Brendan Bowles, here a while ago to get the restaurant going. Have you heard of him?"

I said I hadn't heard of him either.

Cherri's hand flew to her throat. "Oh, he's so good. He trained in France, and this is a French restaurant." She gestured around the room expansively.

At that moment Ted appeared at the table. "Melissa and Marcus insist upon joining us with their business partners," he said in a disapproving tone. He adjusted his tie with his right hand and his cheeks puffed up.

I could see he was embarrassed by my presence, but I really didn't care.

"They'll be joining us soon, Jane, so I'll need you to sign these papers now."

"What papers are they?" I asked him.

"Nothing you'd understand," he said in a derogatory tone. "It's about the family trust." He handed me a bunch of papers.

I immediately put them in my purse.

"Why did you take them? You're supposed to sign them and give them back to me."

I shot him my best fake smile. "Oh Ted, you and I were married all those years and you're a top lawyer. If there's one thing I learned from you, it's never to sign anything without a lawyer looking over it first. No, my lawyer will be having a good look at this."

"And what is the name of your lawyer?" he asked through clenched teeth.

"Never you mind," I said. I noticed Ted's cheeks had puffed out even further and red splotches appeared on his face. Did he really think I was so stupid as to sign something without my lawyer looking at it first? Well, it appeared that he did. I thought he was about to say something nasty when Cherri said, "Here are Melissa and Marcus now."

Ted shot me a nasty look and then hissed, "I'll speak to you later."

"No need," I said with a dismissive wave of my hand. "I'll contact you after my lawyer has viewed whatever you want me to sign."

Two couples arrived at the table at that moment. All four appeared about the same age, although one displayed an inordinate amount of plastic surgery. Her hair extensions did not look at all realistic and she was covered with heavy and garish jewelry. Her plunging neckline left nothing to the imagination and her lace dress was altogether too short. The man with her looked old enough to be her grandfather and was rather portly, with a big, bulbous red nose and a flushed face. If he'd had a beard, he would look like Santa Claus.

The other couple appeared rather more distinguished. The lady was wearing a tasteful blue dress and her husband looked like a distinguished businessman.

Ted wasted no time in doing the introductions. "Melissa and Marcus, I'd like you to meet my ex-wife, Jane…" His voice trailed away. "Jane, do you still have my surname?" His tone was one of a child asking another child if they still had their toy.

I was embarrassed to admit I still did have his name. "Yes, I'm afraid I do," I said with a sigh.

Ted looked quite put out. "Well then, Melissa and Marcus, I'd like you to meet my ex-wife, Jane Delight. Jane, this is Melissa and Marcus Matheson." He turned to the other couple. "Candace and Rick, I'd like you to meet my ex-wife, Jane Delight. Jane, this is Candace and Rick Weatherspoon."

We all exchanged pleasantries. All four of them were looking at me with curiosity plastered all over their faces.

As soon as they took their seats, Candace, the scantily dressed one, leaned forward and said, "How long have you two been divorced?"

"A long time," Ted said before I could answer. "Jane is here tonight because I needed her to sign some papers for me and I very rarely come to Pennsylvania."

Marcus smiled at me. "So how do you like our restaurant so far?"

"It's absolutely beautiful," I said honestly.

"Melissa and Marcus own the restaurant and Candace and Rick are their business partners," Cherri supplied.

I shot her a grateful smile. At least someone had filled me in. The waiter arrived with champagne for everyone. "I hope you like Armand de Brignac," Marcus said, indicating a golden champagne bottle.

I simply smiled at him. My nerves had made me go hot all over—or maybe I was having a hot flush? —and I wanted nothing more than to drink a gallon of iced water. Before anyone could drink the champagne, a man in chef whites appeared at the table. "Brendan," Marcus said. "Everyone, I'd like you to meet the famous Brendan Bowles."

A distinguished man, Brendan gave a half bow while Marcus made the introductions.

"Brendan, please join us for a toast," Marcus said.

Just then, there was a loud sound of smashed glass. We all turned to look. The waiter who had brought our champagne was standing against a wall, looking shocked. Broken glass was lying shattered all over the floor. The customer who had knocked into the waiter hurried away without so much as an apology or a backward look.

Melissa and Marcus looked visibly annoyed, but Marcus recovered quickly.

"I'd like to propose a toast," Marcus said. "To the success of our restaurant!"

They all raised their glasses. I set down my iced water and picked up my champagne glass.

Moments later, Marcus clutched his throat and fell to the ground.

Everyone jumped to their feet. Melissa ran over to her husband. "Call 911," Melissa called out to Ted who wasted no time in doing so.

"What happened?" the waiter said. He was doing his best to shake off Candace, who was clinging to him, her jaw dropped open.

Melissa grabbed his arm and then collapsed into him. "My husband! He's dead!"

Ted looked at me. "This is your fault, Jane!" he exclaimed.

CHAPTER 2

*E*veryone in the restaurant turned to look at me. I clutched my throat and backed away. "My fault?" I repeated. I was in shock.

"Don't be so silly, Popsicle. Of course it's not Jane's fault. Why would you say such a thing?" It took me a moment or two to realize it was Cherri who had come to my rescue.

"*Everything* is Jane's fault," Ted muttered. "I wanted to have a quiet chat with Marcus and Melissa, but we all had to have dinner together simply because Jane was here. They said it was strange they had never met Jane, but I liked to keep my home life separate from work."

I was furious with Ted, but there was no time to worry about such things, what with poor Marcus lying on the floor. Melissa had thrown herself back over him and was sobbing. The chef, Brendan Bowles, was trying to comfort her, but she was pushing him away with her left hand.

Candace and Rick Weatherspoon were standing next to the waiter, all of them visibly shocked. "Are you sure he's gone?" Candace asked. "Maybe someone should try CPR."

Her words were met with a tirade from Melissa. "He's dead! He's dead, I tell you!" She burst into a fresh bout of wailing.

My heart went out to her. I couldn't believe this was happening. I didn't know how long everyone in the restaurant stood there, their mouths open. I wished I could do something to help, but I had no idea what I could do. Mercifully the paramedics arrived quite quickly. They told everyone to back off as they swiftly attended to Marcus.

"Was your husband on any medication?" the male paramedic asked Melissa.

She nodded and reeled off a list of medications.

The paramedics asked Melissa more questions, but I couldn't hear what they said. I had slumped back into my chair, as had Cherri. "It's a terrible thing," she said. "A terrible thing. He was alive only a few minutes ago. I can't believe it."

She was shaking, so I patted her on her back. The paramedics presently told everyone not to leave because the police were on their way.

I gasped.

"What is it?" Cherri asked me.

"Oh, nothing," I said, but I knew that the police wouldn't be called unless the paramedics suspected suspicious circumstances. Cherri reached for her glass, but I put my hand on her arm. "Don't drink that," I said.

"Why?"

"Just in case there was something in it that, err, made Marcus sick," I told her.

Cherri did not appear to make the connection and simply nodded, leaving me alone with my thoughts. Had Marcus been poisoned? I couldn't believe that this was the second person to have been poisoned in a short space of time, and what's more, right in front of me.

What were the odds? Maybe I shouldn't have moved to Lancaster after all. But then again, I was living with two wonderful roommates and I also had the support of my sister who lived on a nearby farm. If I had stayed in New York, I would have been all alone.

I was still trying to remain calm when two

uniformed officers hurried into the room. "No one is to leave until the detectives arrive," one said. "Who was at the table with Mr. Matheson when the incident occurred?"

We all indicated that we were.

"You all need to give your witness statements before you can leave," he said.

"The chef was here too and so was the waiter," Ted told them.

"Names?" the officer barked.

"The chef's name is Brendan Bowles, but I don't know the waiter's name," Ted told him.

"Everyone, move away from the victim!" the male officer said in a commanding tone.

Melissa stood up abruptly. "Victim?" she wailed. The female police officer put her arm around Melissa and somehow managed to maneuver her away from her husband's body.

"I can't believe it!" Ted muttered to himself.

I noticed he hadn't asked Cherri if she was all right and I thought that rather uncaring of him. She was still shaking. I also noticed no one else was touching their champagne, but I took a large gulp of my iced water.

It was lucky I couldn't see the body from where I was sitting and I hoped Melissa would calm down a little now that they had taken her out of the room. The uniformed officers ushered everyone into another room. I figured this was a private room for diners, although no one was dining there when we were all ushered in.

The officer called for attention. "Now I'd like those of you who were at the table with the victim to move over to this side," he said. "The rest of you stay over there. Has anyone noticed anyone leave?"

The consensus was that no one had left, but I remembered the person running away just before Marcus Matheson had fallen to the ground.

I tentatively raised my hand and cleared my throat. The officer swung around to me. "Did you see someone leave?"

"Well, it might not be important..." I began, but he interrupted me.

"Allow me to be the judge of that," he said, although not unkindly.

"Someone knocked into the waiter. It happened before Mr. Matheson, um, died," I said. "Someone knocked into him hard and glass shattered all over the floor. The man took off out the door and didn't even look back or say sorry."

The officer nodded slowly. "And how long was this before Mr. Matheson fell to the ground?"

"Possibly a minute, maybe less," I told him.

He pulled a notepad from his pocket and flipped it open. "Can you describe him to me?"

I shook my head. "It all happened so fast. I only saw the back of him. He was a man and he was only a little shorter than the waiter, but much thicker set. He was about the same build as Mr. Matheson, only like I said, he was taller than him and just a little shorter than the waiter. He had medium brown hair, but that's all I can tell you, I'm afraid."

"That's a better description than most are able to give," the officer said appreciatively. "What is your name?"

"Jane Delight," I told him.

The officer looked past me and hurried from the room.

Ted was still muttering to himself, shooting angry glances my way, for whatever reason I did not know, but at last was now consoling Cherri who was clinging to him with both hands.

The officer walked back through the door. "Will the people who were dining with Mr. Matheson please come this way?"

He led us all through the large room into a smaller room. I had no idea of the purpose of this room, as it was the size of a large bedroom. Against one wall was an Oriental sideboard with a large gilt mirror over it. I idly thought the Oriental sideboard was quite out of place in a French restaurant. I heard someone speak, and I spun around.

Standing there was Detective Damon McCloud and with him, Detective Carter Stirling.

"Not again," Detective McCloud said in his broad Scottish accent.

I could simply offer a shrug.

He sighed and flipped open his notepad. "I need everyone's names please—surname first and Christian name second." He added, "Not you, Miss Delight. I know your name."

Everyone stared at me in surprise and Ted shot me an accusatory look. People gave their names, surnames first and Christian names afterward, and then Detective McCloud came to Ted. He raised one eyebrow.

"Delight, Ted." Ted said.

"I have no idea why you'd be delighted," Detective McCloud said. "I need your name, surname first and Christian name second."

Ted was clearly enraged. "Delight, Ted!" he yelled.

"Why are you delighted?" Detective McCloud

said. "It seems most inappropriate, given the circumstances."

I thought I should explain. "His name is Ted Delight. He is my *ex* husband."

Detective McCloud flushed red. I expect he couldn't quite understand our American accents.

"Quite so, quite so," he muttered, but Ted continued to glare at him.

"Now, we will need to get a witness statement from each of you. You can tell us what happened, in your own words."

"Why would you think we'd use someone else's words?" Ted snapped at him. "I'll have you know I'm a most prominent lawyer."

Ted intimidates most people, so I was pleased to see Detective McCloud was not. He drew himself to his full height, which was taller than Ted, and took a step toward him, looming over him. "Duly noted," he said in an icy tone, although I think it sounded quite cute in his Scottish accent.

Clearly, Ted did not think the accent quite so cute. He took a step backward, but continued to glower at Detective McCloud.

Rick Weatherspoon spoke for the first time since the incident happened. "You obviously suspect foul play," he said. "Should the rest of us be seeking medical treatment?"

"Why would you ask such a question?" Detective Stirling asked him.

"I assume Marcus was poisoned. The food hadn't yet arrived and we all drank the same champagne, so I'm wondering if we all should go to the hospital."

Detective McCloud looked around at all of us, but his eyes rested on me. "Did you all drink the same champagne?"

Everyone nodded, but I said, "I drank iced water. I only took a sip of the champagne when Marcus made the toast."

Detective McCloud took notes. "And no one ate anything else?" Everyone shook their heads. "And you're sure Mr. Matheson didn't drink or eat anything else?" After everyone nodded, he asked, "And how soon after he drank the champagne did he collapse?"

"Quite quickly, probably within seconds, or maybe about a minute," Rick Weatherspoon supplied. "Should we be standing around here if we need medical attention?"

"We don't know if Mr. Matheson was poisoned, but if so, it was clearly a large dose of a fast acting poison," Detective Stirling said. "As no one else is feeling at all ill, this suggests that the poison was meant for Mr. Matheson alone—if it was poison that is. It might simply have been natural causes, but we won't know at this stage. Right now we have to treat it as suspicious, which is why we're asking these questions, but I don't think any of you need to be alarmed."

"Yes, and if Mr. Matheson was indeed poisoned, he might have been poisoned some time ago and not at the dinner tonight," Detective McCloud pointed out. "And as my partner has said, we won't know whether or not it was natural causes for some time. Right now, we'll take witness statements from all of you."

I could hear Melissa crying in another room. It was clear to me the detectives thought Marcus had been poisoned, and I figured from my recent research into poisons that it must have been a large dose of poison. The paramedics clearly thought the same, or they wouldn't have called the police. Yet what poisons acted so quickly?

I knew there was one person who would know the answer, my roommate, Matilda.

CHAPTER 3

J hurried back to my apartment. I couldn't wait to tell Matilda and Eleanor what had happened. I hoped they were back from their dance class. For ladies in their eighties, they certainly were energetic. They put me to shame and I was a good thirty years younger.

I unlocked the door and opened it ever so slightly to make sure that my roommates' naughty cat, Mr. Crumbles, did not escape. He usually waited inside the door ready to slip through.

On this occasion, he was not there, so I let myself in and hurried up the stairs. I was met by loud drum music.

I walked into the living room and gasped. There in front of me, stood a pole from the floor to the ceiling. I gasped. "A stripper pole!" I exclaimed in horror.

Matilda was clearly affronted. "Oh my goodness gracious me, no! It's a dance pole. You knew we were having dance lessons."

I was aghast. "I thought you meant the waltz," I said, scratching my head.

"It's the latest craze," Eleanor informed me. "Many people take pole dancing lessons these days. They say it's good for the core." She muttered to herself, "Not that I know what a core is."

"Won't Rebecca mind? Is it attached permanently?"

Matilda waved one hand at me. "Of course not! It's held on by pressure. It's entirely portable. Would you like to have a go?"

I shook my head.

"Mr. Crumbles might like it," Matilda said. "Cats like poles, don't they?" She picked up the cat and held him next to the top of the pole.

He wrapped his paws around it just as Eleanor screamed. "Matilda! Get Mr. Crumbles off the pole!"

I watched in horror as Mr. Crumbles flew around the pole in a counter clockwise motion, his gray fur flying out in all directions. He picked up speed and then suddenly he was airborne.

The next thing I know I was lying on my back on the ground, winded. As I gasped for breath, I realized what had happened. Mr. Crumbles had let go of the pole and he had been spinning so fast that the centrifugal motion had flung him right off the pole into the pit of my stomach.

Matilda bent over me. "Jane, are you all right?"

I opened one eye just in time to see Eleanor pluck the cat from me. "Oh, you poor thing," she cried, cradling the cat to herself. "I need to get you some cat treats for that. How could you be so irresponsible, Matilda?"

Matilda turned away from me. "He loved it. Kittens enjoy playing."

"Only with balls or toy mice, Matilda. Sometimes I think you act like a five year old child." With that, Eleanor stormed off.

"I'm sorry then," Matilda said. "I'll give him some treats too."

I continued to lie on my back, gasping for air. I had only just managed to sit up when Matilda returned. "Oh, you've gone quite white, Jane. Maybe you were winded."

"I *was* winded," I said. "I wasn't able to breathe for a while."

Eleanor marched back into the room. "There's no need to worry. Everything is under control. Mr. Crumbles has had lots of treats and is quite content."

Matilda rounded on her. "How could you say such a thing? Your cat hurt Jane."

Eleanor held up her hands, palms to the ceiling. "And that's my fault, how? You were the one who put poor Mr. Crumbles onto the pole. I've never seen such an irresponsible act."

Matilda rolled her eyes and was about to say something when I interrupted. "Someone was murdered tonight."

That got their interest. "Murdered?" Matilda asked. "Where?"

"When we were having dinner," I told her

"Was it your ex-husband?" Matilda asked, rather too gleefully. "Are you under suspicion?"

I shook my head and then took a deep breath. "No, it was his client."

Matilda looked disappointed. "Eleanor, help me get Jane off the floor and over to a chair and she can tell us everything."

The ladies grabbed one arm each and pulled

me to my feet. I was surprised at how strong they were. "I'll make Jane a nice cup of coffee to soothe her nerves," Eleanor said over her shoulder as she marched out of the room, Mr. Crumbles trotting behind her.

"Put a lot of sugar in it to calm her nerves," Matilda called after her. "Maybe put some of that brandy in it that you've got hidden in the cupboard."

I could not hear Eleanor's response, and maybe that was just as well.

I sat there until Eleanor had placed the coffee in front of me. I took one mouthful and nearly spat it out. "Did you put any coffee in the sugar?" I said with a laugh.

"You're probably in shock," Eleanor told me, "and sugar is good for shock. Drink it up. Won't you tell us what happened tonight?"

"Ted wanted me to sign the papers as you know," I began, but Eleanor interrupted me.

"You didn't sign them, did you? We told you not to sign them."

Matilda shushed her, but I said, "No, of course not. They're in my purse." I pointed to my purse, which was still sitting in the middle of the room. "Anyway, for some reason the owners of the restaurant and their business partners wanted to have dinner with us. Actually we didn't get as far as dinner, because one of them, Marcus Matheson, drank some champagne and then he pretty much fell down dead."

"Maybe it was a heart attack," Eleanor offered.

I shook my head. "No, the paramedics called the police and the police called the detectives. They said they're treating it as suspicious for the time being."

Matilda arched her eyebrows. "And by detectives, do you mean a certain handsome Scottish detective?"

I tried not to smile too widely. "Yes, Detective McCloud was there. Anyway, I'm wondering what poisons could act so quickly."

Matilda tapped her chin. "Cyanide acts very quickly. Maybe it was cyanide. And strychnine acts quickly too. Did he happen to have severe convulsions?"

I shook my head. "He looked quite peaceable. Well, you know, apart from the fact he was dead."

Matilda nodded slowly. "I see. Apart from all the nerve poisons, most poisons don't act as quickly as that. But as we know from our recent case, maybe the poison was given to him before the incident. Some poisons can be given over weeks before they take their toll."

"Ricin can take a few days to kill," Eleanor said.

Matilda agreed. "Maybe it was tetrodotoxin. Did you happen to eat any puffer fish?"

"I didn't eat anything," I said. "As far as I know they hadn't ordered. Ted, Cherri, and I had ordered but the meals hadn't arrived."

"Cherri!" Matilda and Eleanor squealed in unison. "Cherri was there?" Eleanor added.

"She sure was," I said raising my eyebrows. "Actually, she seems quite nice."

"What does she look like?" Eleanor asked me as she bent down to scoop up Mr. Crumbles.

"She looks like a supermodel," I said. "She's tall and thin and she wears beautiful clothes. She's very young."

"You knew she was young," Eleanor told me, "so that can't have been a surprise. Still, it must have been an awful shock to meet her. Whatever was your ex-husband thinking?"

"Goodness knows!" I said.

"Nerve agents can act quite quickly," Matilda said, apparently losing interest in Cherri for the moment. "And then there is batrachotoxin. Some of it comes from plants, but mostly it comes from the

skins of frogs. A small amount of that can kill you."
Her eyes lit up.

"And there's saxitoxin, don't forget, Matilda,"
Eleanor scolded her. "It's a neurotoxin."

"I was just getting to that," Matilda snapped.
"As our father always said, 'There are two classes of
people who shouldn't see things half done, fools and
children.'"

"I wasn't looking at anything half done though,
was I Matilda? I was listening, not looking. You're
twisting my words as usual."

"So are there any other poisons that act
quickly?" I asked, simply to stop their bickering.

"Oh, yes, botulinum toxin," Matilda said. "It's
one of the most toxic substances known, ten
thousand more times deadly than cyanide. About
one teaspoon could wipe out the world's
population."

I gasped. "You're kidding!"

Matilda took another sip of coffee and then
added, "Yes, it comes in several forms, but it's best
known as Botox."

"Botox!" I exclaimed. "What, are you saying
Botox is made from botulinum toxin?"

Both Eleanor and Matilda nodded sagely. "It
most certainly is," Matilda said. "And then there's

atropine, also known as belladonna," she added, "and of course we all know about wolfsbane."

Matilda leaned over and patted me on my knee. "At least you don't have to investigate this case, Jane. Your sister wasn't even there. She was home with a broken arm, so she's not going to be a suspect, and I doubt you'll be a suspect. You had never met the vic, had you?"

I shook my head. "I never even heard his name before tonight. And I've never even met Cherri. The only person I knew there was Ted."

"And you said you were sitting at the same table as the victim. Were you sitting next to him or opposite him?"

I shook my head again. "I was down at the other end of the table."

"Then you're safe," Eleanor pronounced. "The police can't tie you to this one. We can look forward to a peaceful few weeks of learning how to pole dance and not have to worry about any more murder investigations. I've had enough of murder investigations and snooping around."

"But it was only once," I said, wondering why Matilda was shooting Eleanor a quelling look.

"Once is enough," Eleanor said.

"Yes, thankfully, this has got nothing to do with

you this time," Matilda said, just as the bell to the apartment rang.

"Oh gosh, I hope it's not the detectives," I said clutching my stomach.

Eleanor waved me down. "I'll get it. You stay there, Jane, and recover from your terrible accident." She glared at Matilda.

I was surprised to hear a woman's voice coming up the stairs. I exchanged glances with Matilda.

I was even more shocked when a sobbing Cherri burst into the room.

She ran over and flung her arms around my neck. "Jane darling!" she cried. "Jane, I need your help!"

CHAPTER 4

I stood there with my mouth open, but Matilda and Eleanor flew into action.

"You must be Cherri," Matilda said, raising her eyebrows at me.

I nodded confirmation.

"Eleanor will fetch you some coffee and then you can tell us what's happened," Matilda said.

Eleanor muttered something to herself and hurried from the room.

I managed to detach Cherri's arms from around my neck and patted the couch beside me. "Cherri, whatever is wrong? I can see you've been crying. Tell me what happened."

Eleanor raced back in at that moment with

some coffee. "I put a lot of sugar in it for the shock," she said.

Cherri thanked her before busting into tears. "It's my Ted," she wailed. "The police have arrested him for Marcus's murder."

I was shocked. "Arrested?" I could scarcely believe it.

Cherri shook her head. "Well, not arrested exactly." She dabbed at her eyes with a tissue. "They think he did it."

"And what makes you think that?" Eleanor asked her.

"Because they questioned him for a long time and then Ted told me the police think he did it."

"But what possible motive could he have?" Matilda asked her. "The police do need a motive, you know."

Cherri sipped her coffee and pulled a face. She set the coffee mug down with a clatter. "The police say they have a motive, but Ted says it's all lies, lies!" Her voice rose to a high pitch.

Mr. Crumbles had just come into the room. He fluffed up his tail and fled under the sideboard.

"Let me get this straight," I said, scratching my head. "The police say Ted has a motive for murdering Marcus, but Ted said he doesn't. Is that right?"

Cherri nodded vigorously. "Yes, that's right, darling."

I knew Ted was far from truthful. "What motive is he supposed to have exactly? Do you know?" I asked after an interval.

Cherri shrugged one shoulder. "I don't know, it's gone way over my head. It's something to do with blackmail."

"Blackmail?" I repeated.

"Yes, you know, blackmail. The police think Marcus was blackmailing Ted. Ted could go to prison. They say it's all his fault, but it isn't true!" She burst into tears once more.

Matilda and I exchanged glances over Cherri's head. "But Marcus was awfully friendly with Ted tonight," I pointed out. "It didn't seem as if Melissa or Marcus had a grudge against Ted at all. They were nice to him. Ted also seemed quite friendly with Marcus. If Marcus was blackmailing Ted, then why were the two men on such good terms with each other?"

"Yes, exactly," Cherri said. "That's right! The police are making it up. They just want to have a suspect, so they're pinning it on my poor Popsicle."

I took a deep breath and said in the most soothing tone I could muster, "Now Cherri, the police wouldn't make something up. Someone must have told them this information."

"It's all lies!" she screeched.

"Yes, well, if it's lies, then someone has lied to the police to try to implicate Ted in Marcus's murder," I said. Matilda and Eleanor nodded their agreement.

Cherri spun the coffee cup around. "Oh I see," she said slowly. "So someone is trying to frame Ted."

"Possibly," I said, "but we really don't know enough about it at this point."

"Yes, that's why I've come to see you, Jane darling," Cherri said.

My hand flew to my throat. "Me? You said you wanted me to help you, but I can't see what I could possibly do."

Cherri pouted. "But you were married to Ted."

I was going to say something rude, but I caught myself in time. After all, I knew just what a liar Ted was. "But how can that help?" I said. "Ted needs a lawyer."

"But he *is* a lawyer," she protested.

"Yes, but he needs another lawyer, someone

else," I said patiently. "Someone needs to understand the law to figure out what's going on."

"No, we need someone who has solved a murder before," Cherri protested. "And Jane darling, you and your friends here have already solved a murder."

I gasped. "How did you hear that?"

"I overheard the two detectives talking about it. I can't remember their names. One had a funny accent."

"Aha. Detective McCloud."

She nodded. "Yes, something like that."

"What did they say about me, exactly?"

"I can't remember." She dabbed at her eyes with a tissue once more. "They just said that the three of you figured out what happened with the last murder. Now I'm asking for your help with this murder. I can tell the police aren't going to be any help at all."

"Why don't you give them some time," Eleanor offered. "Give them a week or a month and see what they come up with."

Cherri pouted once more. "My poor Popsicle could be imprisoned by then and awaiting bail." She shook her head. "No, poor Ted entertains me with stories of criminals and now he's been treated as one. Jane, you've got to help me! There's no one else I can turn to. You're my only hope."

I rubbed my eyes with my hand. "Look, I'll do what I can, but I really don't know what I *can* do. I'm running the cupcake store full time by myself now that my sister has broken her arm."

"Eleanor and I can help you with that," Matilda said, earning herself a glare from Eleanor. She turned to her sister. "Oh come on, Eleanor, another investigation will be fun. Don't tell me you don't enjoy investigating."

Eleanor shut her eyes tightly and then opened them. "Okay, I suppose you're right," she said in a weary fashion.

Cherri jumped to her feet and hugged each one of us in turn. She sat back down and drank the rest of her coffee in one gulp. I figured it couldn't be too hot. "All right, what do we do first?"

I shook my head. "I have no idea, to be honest," I told her. "What can we do? And by the way Cherri, I think Ted is going to be very angry that I'm helping you."

"We won't tell him," she said quite happily.

"But he'll find out," I said.

Cherri's eyebrows shot skyward. "How would he find out?"

"We will need to ask him questions at some point, surely."

"No, Jane darling. If you want to ask Ted questions, just ask me and I'll ask him for you. Besides, I'm sure he'd rather answer questions if I asked them. No offense intended."

"None taken," I said dryly. I knew she was right. "Okay then, if you're happy about keeping it from Ted, I suppose we'll have to be happy too."

"Fetch the laptop and make notes," Matilda instructed Eleanor. She scratched her head. "Now what would Miss Marple do first?" She looked up at the ceiling. "Yes, she would gather all the information. Cherri and Jane, I want you to draw a table and chairs and write everyone's name exactly where they were sitting tonight. Also, we need the names of everyone present and the names of any staff who approached the table at any time. Cherri, I don't suppose you know what the poison was?"

"No."

Matilda patted her knee. "Never mind, it's far too soon to know. I was hoping the paramedics had suggested something to the police. We need to know that poison as soon as possible. Now, give me your phone and I'll put my number in your contacts. It won't do if Ted knows you have Jane's number. Tell me, Cherri, does Ted know my name?"

"I don't think he does," she said.

Something occurred to me. "Cherri, how do you know where I live?"

"Ted had your address on the contract," she told me. "I happened to see it when he handed you the papers."

I was a little suspicious. "You must have a good memory."

She shook her head. "I only saw the street name, but I remembered that Ted said that your twin sister has an Amish cupcake store and that you live above it. I drove along the street until I saw the cupcake store."

I nodded slowly. "I see." I wondered if she was telling the truth. I wondered if in fact Ted didn't have a private detective following me after all. Still, I couldn't see what good it would do him, so I figured Cherri was probably telling the truth.

"I put my name just as Matilda in your phone. No surname. Will you remember that?"

Cherri nodded. Matilda punched some keys and then handed the phone back to Cherri. "I just called my number and so I can put your number in my phone. Feel free to call or text me at any time day or night. Do you understand?"

I wondered if Matilda had ever been in the military, because she was certainly quick-witted and good at giving orders.

Cherri looked surprised but nodded. "Thanks for your help, Matilda, but it doesn't matter if I call Jane direct, as Ted never looks at my phone."

Just then, Cherri's phone rang. She almost dropped it with it fright. "It's Ted," she whispered before putting her finger to her lips.

"Where are you, Pumpkin?" Ted's voice said. Cherri had clearly set the phone to Loud. "I've been looking all over for you."

"I'm in the car, Popsicle," she said. "Are you still at the restaurant? I'll go straight back there. I've been driving around because I've been so upset about the police suspecting you. Do they still suspect you?"

"I'm afraid they do." Ted's voice was grim.

Cherri hung up and then turned to me. "Thanks so much, Jane darling. It's so good of you. I'll be in touch." She hurried for the stairs with Matilda on her heels.

"Call us as soon as you know any more, and call

us if you hear what the poison was," Eleanor called after her.

I watched Cherri's departing back. This was the last thing I ever expected, to help my ex-husband who was a suspect in a murder case. I, for one, would be happy to throw him in prison myself.

CHAPTER 5

*I*t was a fun morning at the cupcake store, if you call listening to Matilda recite a long list of fast acting poisons and their symptoms fun. I finally had to ask her to stop.

Eleanor and Matilda had both been helping me in the cupcake store, and they seemed quite good with the customers. I wondered again what the incident was. Rebecca had refused to speak about it.

A regular customer came in to buy five Shoo-fly pie cupcakes. Shoo-fly pies were not normally in cupcake form, but my Amish sister had modified Amish recipes to produce delicious cupcakes. Shoo-fly pies were a concoction of molasses goodness, all sugary and delectable.

When the lady saw Matilda, she gasped. "It's

you!" she said. "If I bring in my calendar, would you both autograph it for me?"

Both Matilda and Eleanor beamed widely. "Yes, but you had better bring it in soon, before Rebecca returns," Matilda told her.

The lady nodded. "Oh, yes, of course. I see." In brighter tones, she added, "I'll bring it in tomorrow!"

As soon as the lady left, I rounded on Matilda. "Okay, my curiosity has finally gotten the better of me. What was this incident that Rebecca doesn't want to talk about?"

Matilda looked at me as if butter wouldn't melt in her mouth. "I don't know what you mean," she said slowly.

I turned to Eleanor. "You'll tell me, won't you?"

Eleanor opened her mouth, but Matilda put her fingers to her lips. "Shush!"

I put my hands on my hips. "I really want to know. Come on, it can't be that bad. I'm going to find out sooner or later, so why don't you just tell me?"

"Your sister really doesn't like talking about it."

"Rebecca isn't here, is she?" I said. "It seems now is a good opportunity for you to tell me what happened."

Matilda let out a long sigh. "It was the cupcake calendar."

"The cupcake calendar?" I parroted. "You'll have to explain a bit better than that."

I held my breath, hoping a customer wouldn't interrupt just when I was on the point of finding out about the mysterious incident. Rebecca kept the details to herself.

"We had the best of intentions," Matilda said. "We were trying to raise money, you see."

Eleanor nodded vigorously. "That's right! All Rebecca's Amish friends were trying to raise money by doing a fundraiser."

Matilda interrupted her. "Yes, because the barn of someone in their community burned down and they were raising money to have a new one built. We were only trying to help."

Eleanor agreed. "It was just before Christmas, so we thought it was a good time of the year to do a calendar for the following year."

Matilda tut-tutted. "Obviously, Eleanor, because it would have been silly for us to do a calendar in the middle of July, wouldn't it!"

I held my hand to forestall the bickering that was sure to follow. "Please just tell me what you did. It surely wasn't that bad."

Matilda looked highly offended. "It wasn't bad at all. I have no idea why Rebecca was so upset." She bit her lip and then continued, "Well, I *can* understand why Rebecca was upset because she's Amish. We should have thought about that, shouldn't we, Eleanor?"

Eleanor nodded. "We should indeed. But we weren't going to sell them to Amish people. We were going to sell them to non-Amish people, and I think we would have sold a lot."

"A lot of these Amish calendars?" I imagined the beautiful Lancaster countryside, cornfields under a golden sunset, or trees dripping with snowflakes, maybe beautiful green fields with buggies being driven across the foreground.

They both giggled. "They weren't Amish calendars, Jane," Matilda said through her chuckles. "But they sold well and we would have sold more, only Rebecca stopped us."

I rubbed my forehead with both hands. "Okay, let me try to piece this together. You two were going to sell calendars to raise money for an Amish barn that had burned down. Is that correct?"

They both nodded.

"And so did you buy these calendars to resell them or did you produce them yourself?"

"We had them professionally printed, of course," Matilda said. "That was our contribution and then we were stuck with them."

"Why were you stuck with them?" I asked slowly.

"Well, because Rebecca wouldn't let us sell any more," Eleanor said. "Luckily we'd already sold enough to cover our costs. They were awfully popular, especially with the old man from the bowling club. He bought a whole box."

"Yes, Eleanor and I took it in turns to take the photographs," Matilda supplied.

I was getting more confused by the minute. "I see, so you took photographs. Did you take photographs of the lovely countryside nearby?"

They both giggled once more. "Not exactly," Matilda said. "Rebecca specifically objected to the photographs."

"Yes, she only objected to the photographs and not to anything else," Matilda said. "What a shame we had to stop selling them."

"Rebecca objected to the photographs?" I asked them. Then I realized what must have happened. I nodded. "Oh yes, I see. The Amish don't like having their photographs taken. The reasons differ from community to community, but the reason in

47

my sister's community is that photos are considered graven images."

I wondered why Matilda and Eleanor looked so surprised, but Matilda said, "No, we didn't take photos of any Amish people."

I was still puzzled. "Then what were the photographs of exactly?"

"Why just of us, of course," Matilda said.

"Rebecca objected to photographs of you and Eleanor?" I asked Matilda.

"Oh yes. We also asked one of the nice young firefighters if we could take his photo and he agreed as well," she said.

"I can't see why my sister minded," I said. "Do you have any idea?"

They both flushed beet red and I wondered why. "Could I see one of the calendars? Do you still have any left?"

"I'll go and fetch you one," Eleanor said. "I have to pop upstairs and check on Mr. Crumbles at any rate. I'll put him at the top of the pole again."

I was horrified. "Why would you do that? I thought you objected when Matilda did it?"

"I did," Eleanor said, shooting a glare at her sister, "but we all gave him so many treats afterwards that now he insists I put up the top of the pole so he can swing down and get treats."

"You're training him badly," Matilda said. "If you didn't give him any treats, then he wouldn't expect you to put him on the pole."

Eleanor was already halfway out the door waving over her shoulder at Matilda.

Before I could pump Matilda for more information, a customer came in and asked for six peanut butter cupcakes. I boxed them, he said, "Oh, I forgot to ask. Do these cupcakes have nuts in them?"

"Yes they do," I said, wondering if my day could get any worse. "They're called peanut butter cupcakes because they contain peanut butter."

"So do they have nuts in them?" the man said.

I simply said, "Yes."

He pushed the box back at me. "I'm sorry, nuts make me sick."

I had been working in the cupcake store long enough that I wasn't even surprised by what the customer had said. I spent another five minutes going through the varieties of cupcakes with him before he finally decided on salted caramel cupcakes.

Eleanor had returned halfway through the

customer looking at each cupcake in the shop. I reached for the calendar she was clutching to her chest. I couldn't understand why Rebecca had objected to the calendar. That is, of course, until I opened the first page.

I gasped and all but dropped it.

"I can't believe it!" I squealed.

"They're rather good photographs, aren't they!" Eleanor said proudly. "I don't know which ones I like the best."

"I like the one of me with the firefighter the best," Matilda said. But then she added in a grudging tone, "Although the November one of you with the firefighter is good too, Eleanor."

"But you're, um, nude!" I stammered, horrified.

Both ladies looked aghast. "We are not!" Matilda shrieked. "We have cupcakes covering our naughty bits."

And they were right. I took a deep breath to steady myself and flipped through all twelve calendar months, each month sporting a photo of Eleanor or Matilda, some with the young firefighter. In each photo, cakes were placed strategically, although I fervently wished there were more cakes, to be honest.

"Don't tell Rebecca you saw it," Matilda said.

"And don't tell her we have any calendars left," Eleanor added. "We would like to frame them and hang them in the apartment, but we're scared Rebecca will see them.

Matilda tapped her chin. "You know, why don't we frame them? We could put them somewhere where Rebecca doesn't go."

"That's a good idea, Matilda," Eleanor said.

I couldn't believe Matilda and Eleanor had produced such a calendar. I shut my eyes and handed it back to Eleanor. I would rather hear symptoms of fast acting poisons than look at that calendar one more time.

I thought it prudent to turn the subject back to murder. "I wonder when we'll hear about the poison?" I asked Matilda.

"Are you having second thoughts about helping Cherri?" she asked me.

"No, I said I'd help and so I'll have to," I said. "It's just that Ted will be furious if he knows I'm helping Cherri."

"Yes, and I know what she said last night," Matilda said. "Cherri doesn't want your ex-husband to know you're helping and she said if you have any questions that she will put them to him on your behalf. However, that's not going to work because of the blackmail."

Eleanor agreed. "Yes, I thought the same thing."

"I might be a little slow, but I don't know what you mean," I admitted.

"Think about it, Jane," Matilda said. "If Ted was actually being blackmailed, then he must have done something bad. Good honest innocent people aren't blackmailed, now are they?"

"No," I said, wondering where this was going.

"Then if Ted was in fact blackmailed, he would have done something he didn't want anyone to know about."

Finally, it dawned on me. "Oh, I see what you mean. If Ted is being blackmailed, he won't want to tell Cherri the bad thing he did that he is being blackmailed about."

"Exactly," both sisters said in unison.

"Then how will we find out what it was?" I asked them.

"I woke up in the middle of the night for a bathroom break you see, and I figured it out," Matilda informed me. "Ted has never seen me, so I'll pretend I'm a private detective and I'll ask him the hard questions."

"But you'll have to tell Ted who hired you," I said.

"Yes, Cherri will have to say she hired a private detective to help him."

I rubbed my chin. "I don't know if she has her own money, and he might not like it. He might be angry with Cherri and object."

Matilda raised her eyebrows. "I get the impression Ted is never angry with Cherri. Jane, you will have to help us convince Cherri."

I shook my head. "I think we'll have a hard job convincing Cherri. She won't believe Ted has done anything wrong."

"Still, it's the only way," Matilda persisted.

Things were rapidly going downhill.

CHAPTER 6

I was hurrying around, preparing to close the store for the day. Matilda and Eleanor had gone upstairs to the apartment to get ready for our visit to Rebecca that afternoon. They had baked her a big freezer meal of macaroni and cheese and I was going to do some baking for her while I was there. I was also going to suggest that Rebecca come and sit in the cupcake store for company, but I didn't know how she'd feel about Matilda and Eleanor helping me. They were doing a good job, but probably the calendar was still fresh in Rebecca's mind. It was certainly fresh in mine.

I was just about to go up the stairs to the apartment when there was a knock on the door. I turned around, about to say we were closed. When I saw Detective McCloud, my heart skipped a beat.

I hurried over to the door and opened it. "Please come in," I said.

"Hello Jane, I mean Miss Delight," he said.

"Please feel free to call me Jane," I said.

Was I imagining it, or had his cheeks turned pink?

"Jane, Jane," he stammered. "I have a few questions about last night."

I nodded. "Sure, go on."

He pulled a notepad and pen from his suit pocket. "In the time that you were married to Mr. Delight, did he engage in any unlawful activities or anything else about which he would be ashamed?"

I nodded slowly. "Oh, I see. You're asking about the blackmail."

He looked shocked, so I hurried to explain. "Cherri, my ex-husband's wife came to the apartment last night because she was upset that someone had falsely accused him of being blackmailed."

"Indeed, the matter has been brought up," Detective McCloud said. "Would you have any insight into the matter?"

"None at all, to be honest," I told him. "I mean,

I was never party to any business dealings of Ted's and I wouldn't even know if he had a gambling problem. All I know is he ran off with Cherri, a college student, and they were having an affair for many months before Ted told me and we separated." I was awfully embarrassed saying all this to Detective McCloud.

Still, I pushed on. "I don't have any idea if he has done anything that he could be blackmailed over. We weren't that close really, although we were married for decades. For more than half the marriage he did his own thing and was never really at home. He did his best to exclude me from his life, so I wouldn't know more than any other person, really."

Detective McCloud nodded slowly. "I see. And was anyone close to the victim last night?"

"What do you mean physically or emotionally?" I said, and then felt quite silly for asking.

"Physically." He looked somewhat amused.

"His wife was sitting next to him the whole time. Are you asking if anyone had the opportunity to pour poison in his drink?"

"What makes you think he was poisoned?"

I groaned. "Come on, it's obvious, isn't it? How

else could he have been murdered? It had to have been poison."

"Did you see anyone close to his champagne glass?"

"His wife was sitting next to him, and Ted was sitting next to him as well. I didn't see anyone touch his glass."

"And his champagne was from the same bottle as everyone else's champagne?"

"Yes."

McCloud raised his eyebrows. "Are you sure of that?"

I nodded. "Yes, I'm certain.

"And did everyone drink the champagne?"

"We all did. I had less than most, but everyone had some."

"And you're certain no food had been served at that point?"

I nodded. "I'm certain. He was poisoned with a fast acting poison, wasn't he? Otherwise you wouldn't ask these questions."

"I'm not at liberty to say," McCloud said although he looked most discomfited.

I couldn't wait to tell Matilda that the poison was fast acting.

Something occurred to me. "You know, the

poison was probably slipped into his champagne during the diversion."

McCloud tapped his pen on his notepad. "Oh yes, when the man knocked into the waiter. Did you actually see them make contact?"

I thought back. "I turned around when I heard the glass breaking. Let me see. The man was already running away from the waiter at the time I looked, and the waiter looked shocked."

"You didn't see them actually make physical contact?" The detective asked me.

I thought that a strange thing to ask. After a moment's reflection, I said, "No, because I only turned around after I heard the glass break and the man was already running away by then."

McCloud nodded. "And did you see anyone else make physical contact with that particular waiter, the one who served the champagne?"

I was about to speak when he said, "Take your time. This could be important."

I wanted to ask why, but I knew he wouldn't tell me. Instead, I ran the previous night scene through my mind. "I can't really remember. I think the women were upset and he was comforting them, but that's all I can remember."

He smiled at me. I noticed the way crinkles

formed at the edges of his gorgeous blue eyes.

"You've been most helpful, Miss Delight, oh, I mean Jane." He added quietly, "And please call me Damon, although not when I'm conducting police business, of course." He shifted from one foot to the other and avoided my gaze.

"Damon," I said with a smile, and wondered when I would actually be in his presence when he wasn't conducting police business. As I was reflecting on that, Matilda and Eleanor burst through the door. Eleanor was clutching Mr. Crumbles.

"What's taking you so long, Jane? We were wondering what was taking you so long," Matilda said, "but now we see for ourselves." She afforded me a big grin, much to my embarrassment.

"Detective McCloud needed to ask me some more questions," I said.

"I bet he did," Matilda said with another wink, this one directed at Detective McCloud.

He looked down and once more fidgeted from foot to foot. "Well, that will be all for now. Good night ladies." With that, he left.

Matilda rounded on Eleanor. "You've brought the cat into the store! And in front of a police officer."

"He's a detective. He doesn't work for the health department," Eleanor said in a rare scornful tone.

"Let's go!" I said. "We're already late."

"Aren't you going to put some make-up on first?" Matilda said.

"I *am* wearing make-up," I said. "Anyway, we're going to visit my Amish sister and her husband. Make-up is the last thing you need to wear to visit Amish folks, surely?"

Matilda looked puzzled, so I added, "I'll just run upstairs and fetch the food I'm taking to her."

"Give me the keys to your car and we'll have the car door open for you," Matilda said.

I shook my finger at her. "I'm driving!"

By the time I had run upstairs, fetched all the food, and grabbed my purse, I was feeling rather hassled. I just wanted to lie down with a cold pack on my forehead and my feet up. It seemed things were carrying me along faster than I wanted them to do.

Mr. Crumbles was sitting at the base of the pole, looking longingly at it. "No you don't!" I said. He meowed pitifully, so I ran back into the kitchen and popped his favorite treat into his cat bowl.

When I got to the car, I found Matilda in the

driver's seat. "Please let me drive," she said in a pleading tone.

I shrugged. "All right, but please drive slowly and within the speed limits."

"I always drive within the speed limits," Matilda said haughtily.

Eleanor made a snorting sound. "That's not true, Matilda. Remember that time we were fleeing from East Berlin…"

I interrupted her. "East Berlin?" I said in shock.

"Hush, Eleanor," Matilda said.

Undaunted, Eleanor pushed on. "Yes, it was before the wall was taken down of course, and we were in East Berlin trying to make a rapid exit."

"That's enough of that," Matilda said. "Jane, you will have to direct me to your sister's farm. I know the way of course, but I might forget."

She most certainly did know the way and I knew she was trying to distract me from asking questions about East Berlin. I had often wondered what these two sisters had been up to in the past, and now I was even more intrigued. Whatever were they doing in East Berlin back in the day, and why had they found the need to beat a hasty retreat? Maybe I would never know.

When we arrived at Rebecca's house, we found

her sitting, reading her German Martin Luther Bible. She looked quite cheery.

"I thought you'd be all forlorn," Matilda said. "How's your arm?"

"It doesn't hurt really," Rebecca said. "Not since it was set anyway, and Sarah Beiler has given me comfrey and arnica tincture to take for healing and bruising."

"*Gut*," I said, lapsing into Pennsylvania Dutch. "Matilda and Eleanor made you macaroni cheese."

Rebecca's face lit up. "*Denki*! Ephraim will be home soon. We will share dinner."

Matilda made to protest, but Rebecca waved her good arm at her. "*Nee*, you must stay and tell us about what happened at the shop today."

"Maybe Matilda and Eleanor would like to prepare the dinner while you and I go over today's sales figures."

Soon Rebecca and I were sipping hot meadow tea and Matilda and Eleanor were making themselves busy in the kitchen. Rebecca seemed quite pleased with the day's takings. "I don't want you to worry about the store, Rebecca," I told her. "It's all under control. Have a good rest."

Just then Ephraim came through the door. "Jane, *wunderbar!*" he said. "It's *gut* to see you.

Thank you so much for helping Rebecca in the store."

"You're most welcome," I said. "Matilda and Eleanor will have dinner ready soon."

He beamed. "*Denki*, I'll just go and wash up."

"We made some extra cupcakes last night for you," I told Rebecca. "We thought we would do some baking here after dinner if that's all right with you."

"*Denki*," she said. "Some of the ladies are coming over tomorrow to clean the house and do some baking."

I nodded. Amish communities were good like that. No one was ever alone, and the community members always helped each other.

"And over dinner, you can tell us all about last night's murder," Rebecca said.

My jaw dropped open. "You know about that already?" I said in shock.

She nodded. "You're aware that Wanda Hershberger's daughter, Waneta, works in the medical examiner's office. Waneta heard all about it and told her mother, and her mother told Susannah Stutzman, who came over and made lunch for us today."

"I was going to break it to you gently," I

told her.

Rebecca frowned. "There's nothing to be worried about, is there, Jane? You're not a suspect this time, are you?"

I let out a big sigh of relief. "No, not this time."

Just then, Matilda and Eleanor walked in. They placed steaming bowls on the table after saying a passing hello to Ephraim.

The five of us sat around the table and bowed our heads for the silent prayer. I said the Lord's Prayer silently as per usual, and then opened my eyes. I bit back a smile when I saw Matilda and Eleanor peeping, each with one eye open. After everyone had helped themselves to large servings of vegetables, mashed potatoes, as well as John Cope's Corn, a baked casserole favored by the Amish, Ephraim asked "What's this about the murder last night, Jane? Are you all right? Rebecca and I are quite concerned about you."

"Yes, I'm perfectly all right now," I told him. "I do feel quite shaken up that everything happened so fast. I haven't had a moment to gather my thoughts." I briefly filled in Ephraim and Rebecca, and then concluded, "And the strangest thing was my ex-husband's wife Cherri came to the apartment last night to ask for my help."

Both Ephraim and Rebecca gasped. "What did she say?" Rebecca asked me.

"Apparently Ted is a suspect. The police think the victim was blackmailing Ted. Cherri wants my help because she thinks I knew Ted better than anyone, even though I tried to point out that I didn't. After all, we pretty much led independent lives before we separated, which became obvious to me only in hindsight," I admitted. "She said she doesn't have anyone else to turn to."

"Do you think it's true that this man was blackmailing Ted?" Jane asked me.

I shrugged one shoulder. "I have no idea, to be honest. Cherri, of course, is convinced that Ted can do no wrong."

"Yes, she seems quite smitten with him," Matilda said. "It's put Jane in a difficult position."

Ephraim nodded. "Yes, it does. What are you going to do, Jane?"

I yawned and stretched. "Have a good night sleep for starters. I really don't know how I can help. To make matters worse, Cherri doesn't even want Ted to know I'm helping her find out who the murderer is."

Ephraim set down his fork. "Jane, please be

careful. It's not good to be mixed up in such matters. You should leave it to the police."

"I really would like to leave it to the police," I told him, "but I told Cherri I'd help her."

"I'm going to pretend to be a private detective," Matilda suddenly announced. "That way Jane will be safe. Jane only has to convince Cherri to tell Ted she hired me. Ted has never met me. I need to interrogate him to see if he was being blackmailed."

Ephraim frowned deeply. "But would he tell you the truth?"

"I have my ways," Matilda said rather confidently.

The talk soon turned to news of the community.

Later that night I was in the kitchen making a beet cake for Ephraim and Rebecca to eat the following day. I was boiling the beets and thinking about what Matilda had said. I didn't want to put Matilda in danger, and I wished I hadn't said I would help Cherri.

Rebecca and Ephraim were reading, while Matilda and Eleanor were cleaning the kitchen even though I had told them that people from the community were going to be cleaning the entire house the following day.

CHAPTER 7

*E*arly the next morning, Ephraim called me from his workshop to tell me that Wanda Hershberger had some information for me.

It was six in the morning and I was on my first cup of coffee for the day. Matilda and Eleanor were already up. Matilda was doing Pilates, and Eleanor was hanging upside down from the pole.

I thanked Ephraim, hung up, and then hurried over to Eleanor. "Are you all right?" I asked her.

"Probably not," she said. "I just can't seem to get this maneuvre right."

Matilda looked up from doing some sort of complicated yoga pose. "You should stretch first, of course."

I wondered how they managed it. After all, I

was decades younger than they were and I couldn't do a complicated yoga pose if my life depended on it.

I at once told them the news. Matilda stood up and Eleanor landed from the pole, her head missing the ground by inches.

"Let's go there right away," Matilda said. "We'll have to hurry to get back in time to open the shop."

"I need my second cup of coffee first," I protested.

Matilda put her hands on her hips. "You're not throwing yourself into this investigation are you?"

"No," I admitted. "I promised Cherri I'd help, so I will. It doesn't mean I have to like it." I took a deep breath and let it out slowly.

"Well, come on then, get ready! I'll make you some more coffee while you get changed."

I threw on some clothes and then staggered into the kitchen, my hand stretched out for the coffee. After the second round of caffeine, I felt better.

I stepped outside into the rain. "I didn't know it was raining," I said. "Where did that come from?"

"The sky, of course," Eleanor said with a chuckle. "Don't just stand there, or you'll get wet. Come on, there's no time to lose. Rebecca will be cross if you don't open the store in time."

Soon we were on our way to Wanda Hershberger's house. Despite Matilda's protest, this time I was driving. "We'll get there much faster if I drive," Matilda said.

"Yes, I'm sure we would," I said with a shudder. "Still, my nerves will remain intact if I drive."

I hoped Wanda wouldn't mind us turning up on her doorstep unannounced, but then again, it was the Amish way to visit with neighbors unannounced. People often called by unexpectedly at dinnertime for a meal. That's just the way it was in the community.

"Hello, Mrs. Hershberger," I said when she opened the door.

"Come inside for some scrapple and *kaffi* soup," she said. "And don't forget to call me Wanda."

I followed the delicious scent of good Amish coffee.

"You got my message then?" Wanda said, before indicating we should sit in the kitchen.

"Yes, we did," I said. Despite my lack of interest in helping my ex-husband, I had to admit curiosity had gotten the better of me. I was intrigued to hear the information.

Wanda hurried around serving everyone. I loved the pork trimmings and the flavors of thyme and

71

sage. Maybe I should change my habits and make scrapple at home instead of having coffee for breakfast every morning.

"How is your *schweschder*?" Wanda asked me.

"*Gut, denki*," I said. "Rebecca said the break was clean, and she's not in any pain."

She nodded. "That's good to hear."

"Surely they haven't got the results on the poison back yet?" Matilda asked Wanda.

Wanda wrapped both her hands around her coffee mug. "*Nee*, they haven't, but I have an interesting piece of information for you."

We all looked at her expectantly, and she pushed on. "A vial of poison was found in the waiter's pocket."

A collective gasp went up around the table. "You're kidding!" I said. "Have the police arrested him?"

Wanda shrugged. "I have no idea. Maybe they have, and maybe they haven't. All I know is, the police told the medical examiner's office to test for the poison in the vial found in one of the suspect's pockets. The medical examiner told my daughter it was the waiter."

"And what poison was it?" I asked her.

"Oh dear, I've forgotten." Wanda scratched

ahead. "Waneta did write it out for you. I'll just go and fetch the piece of paper now. I left it under my Bible. It was something to do with botulism."

"Aha!" Matilda said. She exchanged glances with Eleanor.

Wanda presently returned with a piece of paper which she handed to me. I looked at it, and handed it to Matilda. "Do you know what this is?"

Matilda nodded and in turn handed the piece of paper to Eleanor who gasped.

"Clostridium botulinum. I was telling Jane about it earlier," Matilda told Wanda. "Botulinum neurotoxin is one of the most deadly poisons known," she continued. "Less than a teaspoon would kill the entire population of the world."

"Botox must be a fast acting poison," I said.

"Not necessarily," Matilda said, "it would depend on the dose. If a large amount was injected into the vic or tipped into his champagne, then of course it would kill him quickly. That's why no symptoms were apparent—they didn't have time to appear."

Wanda said, "Botulism? Like in canned food that has gone bad?"

It was Eleanor who spoke. "Exactly. Botulism is deadly and boiling won't kill it. It takes a much higher temperature than boiling water to kill botulism. As you know, Wanda, if preserving fruit is not done correctly, it can cause botulism."

Wanda nodded slowly. "Yes, I do know that. I think everyone who preserves is aware of the danger of botulism."

"And there's wound botulism too," Matilda said. "And you all probably know that infants under one year old are not supposed to have honey because honey can contain a small amount of botulism, just enough to harm a young child."

"I didn't know that," I said. "But if it's so deadly, how would someone procure it?"

"Oh, it's available everywhere," Matilda said with a wave of her hand. Once more, I was shocked. "Have you ever heard of Botox?" she asked me.

"Of course I have," I said. "Botox and botulism are related."

"Yes, but Botox doesn't contain the bacteria. When someone injects someone with Botox, they're actually injecting a tiny amount of the deadly neurotoxin made from clostridium botulinum. Botox is freely available."

I thought that over. "Let me see. Who would

have access to Botox — perhaps plastic surgeons, and beauticians?"

"Botox has medical applications as well," Matilda told me. "So, doctors or nurses would have access to it as well. In fact, when we get home I'll have Eleanor check the laptop and see if it's available without a prescription."

"Surely not," I said. To Wanda, I said, "Did Waneta say anything else?"

She shook her head. "Only that they did test for whatever was in that vial. She also said they're doing the usual tox screenings in case the botulism was a red herring to try to throw them off the track."

"Does, the medical examiner think that's likely?" I asked her.

She shook her head. "*Nee*, my daughter said they think the stuff in the vial poisoned him. Would you like some *kaffi* soup?" Without waiting for me to answer, she broke some pieces of bread into a bowl then poured milk and coffee in it, followed by a slathering of sugar.

"Not for me thanks," I said, "but if you don't mind I'll help myself to some coffee."

When I sat back down with my coffee, Matilda

said, "I find it hard to believe that the waiter did it. Surely he would offload the vial of Botox or whatever form of clostridium botulinum it was before the police searched him. Did the police search you, Jane?"

I shook my head. "No, but they did look in my purse. They searched Ted and the vic's wife." I sighed. Now I was taking to calling victims 'the vic,' following Matilda's example. "And they searched the purses of everyone at the table," I added.

Wanda looked up from her *kaffi* soup. "Yes, surely the murderer would have gotten rid of the evidence first."

"Then that means someone was trying to frame the waiter. So why is someone trying to frame Ted too?" I tapped my head. "Aha! You know, just before Mr. Matheson died, there was a big commotion that distracted us all. Someone knocked into the waiter and ran away. I thought at the time it was very strange because he didn't apologize or even look back. He just took off."

"Could he possibly have slipped the vial into the waiter's coat pocket that time?" Matilda asked me.

"Yes, quite possibly," I said. "You know, when Detective McCloud questioned me yesterday, he asked me if I saw anyone close to the waiter after Mr. Matheson died."

"And did you see anyone?" Eleanor asked me.

"You know it sounds bad, but I really can't remember. The waiter did comfort both the women at the time, Mr. Matheson's wife and their business partner, Candace. I noticed both of them were close to the waiter at different times."

"Who are the other suspects again?" Matilda asked me.

"Ted, Cherri, the waiter, the chef, Mrs. Matheson, Candace and her husband were all present."

"Were they ever close to the waiter?" Matilda asked me.

"I saw the chef patting his back, and I noticed Candace's husband, Rick, bumping into him later and apologizing."

"Did you tell Detective McCloud that?" Eleanor asked me.

My hand flew to my throat. "No, because I was only thinking of the time that Mr. Matheson died. I wasn't thinking of anything that happened after the police came."

Matilda waved her finger at me. "Well, I suggest you call Detective McCloud and tell him that." She sighed. "So to recap, the suspects are the people who were present, your ex-husband and his wife, the vic's wife, the vic's two business partners, the chef, and the waiter, although of all those people I suspect the waiter the least."

"Did you see Ted or Cherri close to the waiter?" Eleanor asked me.

"As a matter of fact, yes," I said. "It's all coming back to me now. Cherri felt faint. The waiter was fussing over her, and then Ted walked over to thank the waiter for his help. They were close enough that Ted could have slipped something into his pocket."

"Could Cherri have slipped something into the waiter's pocket?" Matilda asked me.

"Sure she could have," I said, "but if Cherri is the murderer, then why would she come and ask for my help?"

"Why indeed?" Matilda said, exchanging glances with her sister.

CHAPTER 8

Thankfully, we made it back in time to open the store. I even had time to change into the clothes I wore for work. Eleanor decided to spend some time with Mr. Crumbles, while Matilda accompanied me downstairs into the shop.

As we set out the cupcakes in the display cabinet, I said to Matilda, "Please don't tell me one more symptom of botulinum poisoning. I think I'll faint if I hear any more."

She chuckled. "Okay, if you're sure."

I grimaced. "Yes, I'm sure. You know, I feel quite muddleheaded about this. I know we found out what the poison is and everything, but I just don't feel I am thinking straight about this murder, not like the last one."

"Last time you were a suspect," Matilda said, "and this time it's your ex-husband who is a suspect. I'm sure you don't have the best of feelings toward him, so it would be clouding your judgement."

I imagined Ted in prison for years. I imagined him in a small exercise yard and then locked up in solitary confinement. I gave a half-hearted smile as I arranged some popping candy cupcakes on a tray. As I set out the plate of sample cupcakes, I said, "This reminds me of when Colin Greaves was murdered after he ate one of these cupcakes."

"But the poison had nothing to do with the cupcakes," Matilda reminded me. "It happened well before that."

I waved one hand in the air. "Sure, I know that. It's just that it reminded me, that's all. I suppose we should make a methodical plan and go through the suspects one by one."

"Let's do that after work today," Matilda said. "We can do it while we're baking the cakes."

"I was hoping to bake plenty of cupcakes in the downtime today," I told her, "but either way, it will be good to make a list of suspects tonight."

Matilda readily agreed. "And we can go through

them one by one. You know, it would be a good idea if maybe we could first focus our efforts on how someone could possibly obtain Botox. Would you happen to know if Cherri is a nursing student? Or rather if she was before she married Ted?"

I shrugged. "She was a college student. I have no idea what classes she took."

"What about the vic's wife or his business partners? Maybe the waiter or the chef are former nurses? Maybe one of them has a relative who works in a hospital." Matilda had a faraway look in her eyes. Suddenly, she exclaimed, "I know! Be right back." Before I could do a double take, she had disappeared out the door.

I had only just finished setting out all the cupcakes and flipped the sign on the door to Open when Matilda hurried through the door. "Honestly, my sister can be so irritating at times." Her expression was grumpy.

"Why, what did she do now?" I asked her.

"It seems her little cat enjoys swinging on that pole," she said. "Rather, I'm sure he doesn't enjoy it, but she gives him so many treats when he lands that all he wants to do is go up on the pole."

I scratched my head. "You know, I wouldn't have believed it if I hadn't seen for myself."

Matilda shook her finger at me. "And that's not all! Did you know he flew off again and narrowly missed my head? He missed me by this much." She held her thumb and forefinger apart about an inch. "He went flying past my head. I'm sure he did it deliberately. And when I told that sister of mine that she can't keep picking him up and putting him on the pole, she said the most ridiculous thing. Would you like to guess what she said?"

I shook my head. "Not really."

Undaunted, Matilda pressed on. "She said she would put his cat activity tree next to it so he could reach the top of the pole by himself. Have you ever heard such a silly thing?"

I tried to picture it. "I don't think it's such a good idea," I said.

Matilda shook her head in disgust. "I agree. Anyway, back to our murder investigation."

The door opened at that point and a deep male voice said, "Did you just say *your* murder investigation?"

Matilda flushed beet red, as did I looking at Detective McCloud, although I knew we had different reasons. "Oh, did I say that?" she sputtered. "I meant your investigation of course."

Detective McCloud crossed his arms over his chest. "I hope you're not thinking of investigating."

"That would be silly, wouldn't it," Matilda said. "After all, we're not suspects this time. It's only Jane's ex-husband and I'm sure Jane doesn't want to help him."

McCloud raised his eyebrows and looked at me. "You don't want to help your ex-husband?"

I shrugged one shoulder. "Not particularly, to be honest. I do feel sorry for Cherri though."

"You feel sorry for your husband's wife who was his mistress when you were married to him?" Detective Stirling said. I hadn't even noticed him come in. Either I was completely entranced by Detective McCloud, or Detective Stirling was sneaky.

"Yes, I really don't care who he marries these days," I said with a dismissive wave of my hand. "I do feel sorry for Cherri because she's young and who knows—he could abandon her one day."

"Yes, it's always awfully difficult after a marriage breakup," Matilda said. "Are you married, Detective McCloud?"

Detective McCloud looked decidedly uncomfortable. "Not anymore."

"Are you divorced too?" Matilda asked him.

He shook his head. "No, my wife passed away some years ago."

"Let us ask the questions," Detective Stirling said in a brusque tone. "I don't think our personal lives are of any concern to you."

"So what can we do for you?" I asked them.

Stirling flipped open his notepad. "Mrs. Delight," he began, but I interrupted him. "It's Miss, obviously. As you are well aware, my ex-husband has remarried."

"Yes, I should know it's Miss by now," Stirling countered, "since you have been involved in two murder investigations in a short space of time."

I bristled. "I hardly think *involved* is the right word, Detective," I said. "It was proven I had nothing to do with the last murder, and this time I was simply a witness."

Stirling made to speak again, but Detective McCloud forestalled him. "That's right. Now Miss Delight, we would like to ask you some questions about your ex-husband, Ted Delight. Was he always a lawyer? By that I mean, was he a lawyer straight out of college or did he perhaps train in medicine, or anything else?"

I shot Matilda a look. "No, he's always been a lawyer," I said.

"And what about his wife, Cherri Delight?" Stirling asked me. "What do you know about her?"

"I met her for the first time the other night," I told him. "I hadn't even spoken to her on the phone before that. The first I knew of her was on my fiftieth birthday when my husband told me he was leaving me and marrying Cherri. All I knew was that she was a college student. I have no idea if she was studying brain surgery or what she was studying."

Stirling looked disappointed. "And did your husband have close friends?"

"I suppose so," I said, "but he never brought them home and he never took me out to dinner with any of them."

"Did he have more than one mistress?" Stirling asked me.

I shrugged. "I don't have a clue. Cherri is the first one he told me about, but he could have had more for all I know."

"Thanks for your help, Miss Delight. I'm sure we'll speak again," Stirling said.

He and Detective McCloud made to leave when Cherri burst through the door. She let out a screech when she saw the detectives. "What are you two doing here?" she said in a high-pitched tone.

"I could ask you the same thing," Stirling said. "Are you friends with Miss Delight?"

"We're not exactly friends, but she seems like a nice person," Cherri said. She was wide-eyed, looking like a deer caught in the headlights.

I thought I had better explain before the detectives thought Cherri and I were in it together and added me to the list of suspects. "That night after Mr. Matheson died, Cherri came to the apartment and said she was very upset that her husband had been questioned over the murder."

Stirling narrowed his eyes. "That seems a strange thing to do considering she never met you before."

I opened my mouth to say something, but Matilda beat me to it. "Cherri said she didn't know anyone else in town and she was awfully distraught," Matilda told him. "My sister Eleanor and I were with Jane when Cherri came in. We were all surprised to see her, considering Jane had met her for the first time that night, but Cherri said she had nowhere else to go. She was upset that you suspected her husband."

"And why would you be concerned that we would suspect your husband was involved in the murder?" Stirling said to clearly frightened Cherri.

"Because you questioned him a lot," she said. "He didn't do it, I tell you!"

"And what are you doing here now?" Stirling asked her.

"Because Ted was questioned again this morning!" Cherri's voice rose to a high pitch. "I don't know anyone else in town, but Jane has been nice to me. I don't know what to do." With that, she burst into tears.

Matilda hurried over to her. "Can't you see you're upsetting the poor girl, Detective? She has no doubt come here again for some more sympathy. Like she said, she doesn't know anyone else in town and she's a long way from home."

Stirling narrowed his eyes once more. "I'm sure we'll want to speak with you again soon, Mrs. Delight."

I was about to correct him automatically when I realized he was speaking to Cherri this time.

Detective McCloud shot me a sympathetic look before following his partner out of the door.

Cherri abruptly stopped crying, which made me wonder whether they had been crocodile tears. "The police questioned me earlier."

"What did they ask you?" I said.

"They asked me if I have regular Botox

injections or filler. I mean, the nerve of them! Why would they want to know about that? Sure I've had several procedures, but I can't see what business it is of theirs. It's an invasion of privacy!"

I was wondering whether we should tell her about the Botox, but Matilda clearly thought we should. "You have to keep this to yourself Cherri, but we found out what the poison was."

Cherri gasped. "What was it?"

"Clostridium botulinum," Matilda said.

Cherri looked blank, so I thought I had better explain. "That's like Botox," I said. "Botox is a deadly poison. It's like botulism without the bacteria. You know, in bad food."

Cherri nodded. "Yes, I know what Botox is, Jane darling," she said. "I have it on a regular basis."

I was surprised that someone so young would feel the need to have Botox. "Oh I see," was all I said.

"The detectives were just here asking about your background," I told her. "We didn't let on to them that we knew the poison was clostridium botulinum, but I'd say they were trying to find out if you or Ted had any medical background. Did you study nursing at college?"

Cherri laughed softly. "Oh no, I was a fashion major. I would faint at the sight of blood."

"They're obviously trying to see how someone could obtain Botox," Matilda said and then clamped her hand over her mouth. "I forgot! That's what I was coming downstairs to tell you when the detectives came and it went completely out of my mind."

"Well, what was it?" I prompted her.

"I asked Eleanor to stop playing with Mr. Crumbles for a few moments and find out if it's possible to buy Botox online without a prescription."

I rubbed my neck. It had been sore lately, most likely from me tossing and turning in my sleep. "Surely not! Wouldn't someone need to be a doctor or a nurse or at least a beautician to gain access to it?"

Matilda practically bounced up and down on the spot. "No! I was shocked too, but you can buy it online. In fact, Eleanor clicked on some injectable solution as well as some Botox powder and put it in her shopping cart. It didn't ask her for any medical qualifications at all. It's in another country and they do ship here. Plus, Eleanor found out that due to different regulations, it's much easier to get it in some states than others."

I was shocked. "I can't believe such a deadly poison would be so accessible to the public," I said.

Matilda appeared unperturbed. "Anyone could be killed a dozen times over from plants in the garden."

"Then anyone could have poisoned Marcus, anyone at all," Cherri said. "I don't see how that helps Ted." She looked as though she was about to burst into tears, and I could see some regular customers heading our way.

"Matilda, why don't you take Cherri upstairs and make her some coffee?" I asked.

Cherri at first was reluctant to leave. "Have you found out anything else about the case?" she asked us.

"We found out the poison," I said, "and please don't tell anyone that we know."

"I won't," Cherri said.

"And tonight we will make a list of all the suspects and then we will investigate them one at a time," Matilda told her.

Cherri suddenly smiled. "I suddenly feel better. I won't need coffee after all. I have a great idea."

A sensation of dread at once hit me. "What is it?" I asked tentatively.

"Leave tomorrow night free." With that, she hurried out the door.

Matilda turned to me. "That sounds ominous."

CHAPTER 9

The morning had gone slowly, but by lunchtime, the customers came in droves. I was grateful I had been able to get the bulk of the baking done earlier. Both Matilda and Eleanor helped me serve customers. Matilda disappeared mid afternoon saying she had a bright idea. That made me somewhat uneasy, even more uneasy than Cherri's similar proclamation. Things did not improve when she returned.

"I've been doing some research. I called Cherri and asked her to call Candace Weatherspoon to ask for the name of the clinic where she has fillers and Botox."

"That's great," I said. "I wonder if she'll be able to find out."

Matilda shot me a sly smile. "She's already found out. Isn't that wonderful!"

"Oh yes," I said, wondering why a feeling of impending doom suddenly beset me.

"Actually, I have her doctor's name and what's more, I've made an appointment for you this afternoon. Isn't that great!"

I gripped the countertop with both hands. "You're not serious, are you?"

Matilda smiled and nodded. "You don't have to have Botox or anything. The first consultation is free. Just go there and ask questions."

"But what questions could I possibly ask?" I said. "What possible good would it do for me to go there?"

"Well, we don't know, and that's precisely why you have to go," Matilda said as if it was the most logical thing in the world to say. "Snoop around the clinic—see where they keep the Botox. Who knows, you might even overhear something. Ask the doctor about the dangers of Botox. You could even ask if someone has to be licensed to administer it. I know, you could say that a local esthetician offers Botox and why is it safer if the doctor administers it, that sort of thing."

My head was already spinning. "I don't like the sound of this, Matilda. I don't like the sound of it at all."

"I can't believe our luck booking you in this afternoon," she said. "I told the receptionist Candace Weatherspoon recommend the clinic to you."

"What if the clinic finds out she didn't?" I asked her.

Matilda popped a sample cupcake into her mouth and chewed it slowly. After she finished, she said, "Never you mind. Candace is unlikely to go there today. You're perfectly safe."

I wrapped my arms around myself. "I'm not sure I like this sleuthing business," I told her. "I'd never make a detective or a private detective at that."

"Oh, you'll be fine," Eleanor said as she entered the room, clutching Mr. Crumbles.

"Eleanor, you know you can't have a cat in the shop," I said. "What if the health inspector sees him?"

"He's lonely, that's all," she said. "We've all been in the shop all day, and he's not used to it. There's been no one to spend time with him."

"Well, I'm sure Matilda and I will be all right by ourselves, so you go and spend time with Mr. Crumbles," I said, making shooing motions with my hands.

Thankfully, Eleanor and Mr. Crumbles disappeared through the door, although Mr. Crumbles did shoot me rather a dirty backward glance.

I wasn't looking forward to having the appointment with the plastic surgeon, so it was with great trepidation Matilda and I drove to the clinic.

"It looks awfully posh," I said.

"Look, you're wearing your best clothes," Matilda said. "Don't worry about it. What's the worst that could happen?"

"He might stab me to death with a syringe of Botox," I said.

For some reason, Matilda thought I was making a funny joke and clutched her sides laughing.

"Matilda, I'm really nervous," I said. "I'm quite scared about this."

"The first consultation is free, like I said," Matilda said. "Just go in there and say you've never had plastic surgery before and you're scared of having it. Ask what he can do for you."

I let out a long sigh. "Okay. Suppose it can't be too bad." I was trying to convince myself more than anything.

When I walked over to the receptionist, her face startled me. I had never seen skin so tight on anyone before, and her eyebrows hung at an unusual angle. "I'm Jane Delight, here for Dr. Davidson at six," I told her.

She stared at me. "You haven't been here before, have you?"

"No."

She handed me a clipboard with a bunch of papers on it. "We like all new patients to fill out their medical history first. That's why we asked you to come five minutes early. Just bring it back here when you're finished." With that, I was dismissed. She looked down and tapped away at her phone.

I sat next to Matilda and filled out the usual paperwork—name, date of birth, address, any allergies, any medications and so on.

When I completed it, I took it back to her.

This time she thanked me but didn't look up. "Dr. Davidson will be with you presently."

She had a strange idea of 'presently', because I waited another fifty minutes before I was summoned into Dr. Davidson's consulting room. It looked more like a spa than a medical office.

Dr. Davidson clearly partook of his own services. I had no idea of his age because his hair was colored brown with golden highlights. It was that type of brown hair color that cannot be natural, and his eyebrows were an even darker shade of brown and were rather a nice shape. His skin too was quite tight, and he had very sharp cheekbones. His nose was paper thin, so thin I wondered if he could even breathe properly.

Dr. Davidson indicated that I should sit and then flipped through my notes. I took the opportunity to study the room. No vials of medication were on display.

"So, obviously you've never had any work done," he said.

"That's right," I said.

"Do you mind if I ask why now, at your age?" He said, with only the slightest hint of disdain.

"Well, my husband left me and ran off with a younger woman," I said. It was the first thing that came into my head, and I figured it would be believable.

Dr. Davidson nodded sagely. "Quite so, quite so. And when did this happen?"

"It was several months ago now," I told him. "Almost a year."

"Ah, what a shame you didn't come to me sooner, much, much, much sooner."

I glared at him, wondering how many more times he could say, 'much'.

He was still speaking. "I advise people to start procedures at a much, much, much younger age than yours."

I shifted uncomfortably in my seat. I had been raised Amish, and we didn't even have mirrors, apart from the small mirrors the men used for shaving. Consequently, when I had entered the non-Amish world, I wasn't accustomed to the concept of vanity, but I must admit I had become somewhat vain over the years. His mention of my age made me squirm. Unfortunately, he continued.

"So how old are you now?" He consulted his notes. "I see. Almost fifty-one years old." He tut-tutted. "It is rather an *advanced* age to be starting procedures."

I scowled at him, but then remembered I was there under false pretenses.

He looked up and must have caught my expression because he hastened to add, "Well, it's never too late to start. I'll make you look a lot younger." He sighed and wiped his brow. "Actually, with you, I don't know where to start. There's so much to be done. Obviously, we need to lift your eyes, and then you…" He broke off and consulted his notes once more.

I was rather offended. I think he thought every part of me needed to be remodeled.

"I'm quite afraid of surgery," I said. "Couldn't I start with nonsurgical procedures first and then work my way up to it when I got a bit braver?"

He shook his head. His expression was grim. "I'm afraid fillers and Botox can only do so much for a woman of your age who has never had procedures before." He cast me a sad look.

I fought the urge to run out of the room. "So Botox won't help me?"

His face lit up. "On the contrary, it will help you very much. It will help your sagging jawline and the fine lines around your mouth and your eyes. I assume you did a lot of crying after your husband left you?"

I nodded.

He pushed on. "Yes, it shows on your face. It's best to avoid crying and smiling, really."

"I see," I said. "And would you recommend fillers or Botox or both?"

"Both, of course," he said.

He stared at me, and a heavy silence fell. I felt I should say something. "Does it hurt?"

"Not really," he said, "but beauty always hurts. That's the price we have to pay now, isn't it?"

"I suppose so," I said. "I've heard Botox brings excellent results. My friend, Candace Weatherspoon, told me that."

"It's a shame you didn't take her advice sooner," he scolded me.

"Um, yes, yes," I stammered. "However, I've noticed there are some estheticians who also offer Botox at quite a low price. However, I've heard it can be dangerous, so I assume it would be much safer to go to you for the procedure."

"Most definitely," he said.

I could see he wasn't going to be forthcoming, so I tried to draw him out. "And will I be in any danger from Botox?"

"There are dangers in everything," he said, "although far less from a skilled practitioner such as myself. Read this information to inform yourself." He pushed some papers across the desk at me and tapped them.

"So, could it be dangerous?"

"Yes, it could be dangerous," he said, "and there

might be some unpleasant side-effects. Sometimes one side of the face is paralyzed and not the other. Of course, I'm highly experienced so you don't need to worry."

I could see he was only interested in the cosmetic implications. I added, "But can it kill you?"

He was so surprised he gave a little start. "Goodness me, I certainly hope not! Is that what you're afraid of?"

I nodded. "I'm sure you'll think I'm silly," I said, "but I have heard of people dying from botulism."

He laughed in an overly condescending manner. "No, it's quite safe in the small amounts we give it. There are no bacteria in Botox."

I could see this appointment was a complete waste of my time. There were no bottles of Botox in his office. In fact, I couldn't see any products at all. I had gained nothing by visiting him. He could only cast aspersions about my age. I racked my brains trying to think of something else I could ask him. "So after someone has lots of Botox and dermal fillers from you, maybe after a few years, do you give them Botox and fillers to inject into their own faces at home?"

He looked shocked. "No, not at all. That would be most inappropriate as they wouldn't have the skills to do it."

My theory was busted. I had visions of Candace pretending she wanted Botox and taking home a few vials so she could poison Marcus Matheson.

"Well, it's certainly a lot to think over," I told him. "What do you think I should have first?"

"I'd suggest dermal fillers, Botox, microdermabrasion, and laser skin resurfacing treatments at least. And that's just for starters. Later you can have a face lift, rhinoplasty, neck and eyelid surgery, brow lift, and a forehead lift." He smiled and rubbed his hands together gleefully. "You do need a lot of work, you understand."

I stood up. "Thanks, I think, Dr. Davidson. All right then, I'll be on my way." I clutched the information sheets and hurried out of the consulting room. I'm sure he wanted to tell me more, but I just didn't want to hang around and listen.

I walked back to Matilda in the waiting room. "How did it go?" she asked me. I merely shook my head.

When we were outside and safely out of

earshot, I told her what had happened. "And so it was a complete waste of time," I concluded. "The only thing I found out was that he never gives anyone Botox or dermal fillers to inject into themselves at home, but we'd already figured that out for ourselves. The whole thing was a complete waste of time," I repeated.

Matilda waved a finger at me. "Not quite. I had a snoop around the clinic, and I found the room where they keep their medications."

I was shocked. "How on earth did you do that, Matilda?"

"I asked where the bathroom was and went into the wrong room. Of course, a nurse told me to leave immediately, but I got a good look first."

"Did you see where the Botox was?" I asked her.

"I didn't get close enough to read the label, but I saw some bottles of medication."

"Do you think someone could slip in and steal any?"

"Well, they certainly saw *me* trying, and I'm quite good at sneaking around," she said. "Besides, I noticed the cabinets were locked."

"So if Candace is the murderer, it's unlikely she acquired her Botox from here."

Matilda agreed. "It *is* most unlikely. However, the murderer probably bought it online. I mean, if we found where to source it fairly quickly, then someone who is intending to murder someone with Botox would find the same thing."

CHAPTER 10

I arrived home feeling somewhat deflated that the plastic surgeon thought I was a train wreck. Matilda had done her best to cheer me up in her own way.

"I don't know why you're so upset," Matilda said for the umpteenth time. "Amish aren't supposed to be vain."

"But I haven't been Amish for years now," I protested, "and it did hurt my feelings, to be honest."

"But Amish don't even have mirrors, do they?" Matilda said. "If you're upset, just don't look in a mirror."

I shrugged. I might as well hold my breath.

Matilda opened the apartment door while still talking to me. I reached out to grab the door handle to prevent it from opening further. I always opened it a little at a time so Mr. Crumbles wouldn't make a dash for it, but Matilda must have been so engrossed in lecturing me about vanity that she wasn't thinking.

A gray streak ran through Matilda's legs, setting her off balance. I grabbed her arm to steady her and then shrieked, "Mr. Crumbles!"

"Eleanor is going to kill me!" Matilda said. She took off after the cat, leaving me standing with my mouth open. I had no idea Matilda could run so fast.

I took off after her. To my enormous relief, Mr. Crumbles was sitting on the sidewalk. Matilda bent down to pick him up, but as her hands were only inches from him, he took off again.

Once more, we gave chase. There were some houses not far from Rebecca's shop. Mr. Crumbles jumped the gate and ran into someone's garden, sprinted to the front door, and disappeared from view.

"Where did he go?" Matilda cried.

I pointed to the large dog door in the front door. "They have a dog door," I said. Both of us let ourselves in through the front gate and ran up the path.

"This is Mr. Cheever's house," Matilda said. "He has a Beagle." She banged on the door. "Mr. Cheever? Mr. Cheever? It's Matilda Birtwistle. Are you home?"

After the fifth time she had yelled his name, we concluded he wasn't home. "He must be out walking his dog," Matilda said, "because the dog barks a lot and so we'd know if his dog was inside."

"What are we going to do?" I asked Matilda. "I suppose we could sit here and wait until he comes home."

"But what if he's visiting his son in Florida?" Matilda said. "He visits him several times a year. I know, I'll peep through the dog door." She bent down and looked through. I heard a muffled sound and then a yell.

"What happened?" I asked her when she emerged.

"That naughty cat is sitting just out of reach," she said. "When I reached for him, he swatted at my hand. He thought it was a joke."

"Call Eleanor and ask her to bring his treats," I said.

Matilda shrank back. "Eleanor will kill me," she said again.

"Look, we really don't have much choice."

Matilda pointed to the door. It was quite a pretty door, freshly painted in pale powdery blue, contrasting with the old, tired beige walls of the house. "You try, Jane. You're taller and skinnier than I am, so you might be able to reach Mr. Crumbles and pull him out."

I was doubtful, but I didn't see I had a choice. "Okay," I said with a resigned sigh. I bent down and shimmied through the dog door. Indeed, Mr. Crumbles was sitting there. Was it my imagination, or was he smirking at me? He certainly seemed to be enjoying the scene unfolding before him.

"Here kitty, kitty," I said in what I hoped was an encouraging tone. "Come here, Mr. Crumbles."

Mr. Crumbles just sat there glaring at me. Granted, it was his regular expression, but he made no move toward me.

"Come along, nice kitty," I said again. This time Mr. Crumbles walked a couple steps toward me.

I stretched out my hands for him, but he was just out of reach. Since he didn't look like he was going anywhere, I put one hand on the ground and with the other hand lunged to him. In what was excellent timing on his part, he waited until my hand was ever so close before sprinting away.

"He's run away," I called out to Matilda. I tried to shimmy backward, but I was stuck. On my next attempt, I realized my hips were firmly wedged in the dog door. The edges of the dog door dug into me. "Help!" I cried to Matilda. "I'm stuck!"

The next thing I knew two hands were on my ankles pulling me. Apart from the fact it felt like a nice physical therapy session for my spine, it did absolutely no good.

"It hasn't helped," Matilda said, echoing my thoughts. "You're well and truly stuck."

"I know I'm stuck," I said. A moment of panic hit me. Would emergency services have to come and cut me out of the door? All sorts of horrible possibilities flashed through my mind.

"I'm making some calls," Matilda said, her voice fading away. I heard her footsteps walking away from the door.

"Don't leave me," I wailed. Mr. Crumbles had come back and was sitting just out of reach once more, looking at me. "I can't believe you did that," I said to him.

He just sat there, frowning at me.

Presently I heard Matilda's voice again. "Don't worry, I called Eleanor to bring his treats. She was awfully angry with me and said... Well, never mind what she said. It wouldn't be good to repeat it in polite company. Anyway, she'll be here soon with the cat treats."

"But what good will that do, because I'm stuck in the door? Help me!" I yelled.

"There's no need to worry. I've called the firefighters."

My blood ran cold. "No, Matilda, please cancel them."

"But how will we get you out?"

"Just pull a bit harder," I said. "I'd be embarrassed if the firefighters came." I closed my eyes tightly and tried to imagine the scene that would greet them with the end half of me stuck out the door. "Pull harder!" I screeched.

"Don't worry. When Eleanor comes, we'll take a leg each," Matilda said.

I didn't know if that was supposed to comfort me or not.

"Oh look, here she is now."

I could hear talking in muffled tones and then I heard Matilda cry, "Ready!"

Hands gripped my feet and then pulled hard. "It hurts," I whimpered.

"Honestly Eleanor, you weren't supposed to pull at the same time as I did. I told you we should take it in turns to pull on a leg."

"I don't recall you saying that," Eleanor said. "When did you say that?"

The next thing I knew they were taking turns pulling on my legs. "It's not working," Matilda lamented loudly.

They stopped talking for a while and I wondered what was going on. Mr. Crumbles hadn't moved an inch. He was staring at me as if he was watching a good movie on TV.

I heard a male voice. The owner of the voice apparently knew Eleanor and Matilda as they all seemed excited to see each other.

I wondered where they had met and then it finally hit me. Oh no! I bet it was *that* firefighter! Dreadful memories of the calendar flashed through my mind.

"Don't worry, Miss Delight, we'll have you out of there in no time," said the male voice. "I'm going to try to wedge you out."

He pulled hard on my legs, but nothing happened. "Don't worry, I'll have you out in no time," he said again. I then heard him add more quietly, "It doesn't look good at all. I think she's firmly stuck."

To me, he said loudly, "Can you edge forward at all?"

"No, I'm stuck," I said. I should have thought that was obvious.

"Let me explain," he said. "If someone is trying to remove a fence post from the ground and it's stuck, sometimes it helps to hit the post on the top of the head with a mallet. That's what we're trying to do with you."

I rubbed my forehead. His reasoning entirely eluded me, but I did try to edge forward a little. "I don't know if that helped," I said.

Eleanor piped up. "Will the butter help now?"

"It's worth a try," the firefighters said.

I could now hear Eleanor's voice close to me. "I'm going to try to push butter around the edge of the door. It might feel horrible."

"I don't care how it feels," I said wearily. "As long as it helps."

Still, the butter was cold and did indeed feel quite unpleasant oozing through my clothes.

"Good job, Eleanor," the firefighter said. "Now

Miss Delight, I'm going to make another attempt to free you. Are you ready?"

"Yes, I am."

The next thing I knew, I was flying backward through the door. I lay there dazed on the porch looking up at the potted plant above. "Thank you," I said.

"Always happy to help a relative of my good friends, Matilda and Eleanor," the firefighter said.

"But I'm not..." I began, but he interrupted me.

"I can tell you're related by your bottom."

My jaw fell open, and I struggled to my feet. "We're not related," I told him. "And why aren't you in uniform?"

"We called Gene on his private cell phone," Matilda said, frowning as if I had said something rather silly. To the firefighter, she said, "Thanks so much for your help. I didn't know what we would have done if you hadn't come to our aid."

I struggled to my feet in time to see Eleanor up to her waist in the dog door. Luckily, she was far skinnier than I was. She soon emerged clutching the little cat to her. "Poor Mr. Crumbles, poor Mr. Crumbles," she said. "What a terrible time you've had. My sister will have to be more careful." She shot Matilda a dark look and stormed away, still clutching Mr. Crumbles to her.

He looked over her shoulder at me. I was almost certain he smiled.

CHAPTER 11

*M*atters did not improve at all. Cherri had called and revealed her surprise. It was more a shock than a surprise. Candace was having a Botox party at her house that night. Cherri was invited, and she had wrangled an invitation for the three of us.

Matilda was excited, saying it was a good opportunity to study two of the main suspects, Candace Weatherspoon and the vic's wife. I agreed it was an excellent opportunity in theory, but I didn't want to have another experience with Botox. Still, I supposed it was inevitable since it was the poison in question and I was supposed to be investigating.

I spent the whole day dreading the Botox party.

After a particularly difficult customer left, I said to Matilda, "I don't see how I can go to a Botox party and not have Botox."

"I'm certainly getting some," Matilda said. "We don't want to blow our cover, now do we?"

I gasped. "You're actually going to have Botox at the party?"

She shrugged. "Why not? It might help my face." She patted her face and then laughed. "I'm only joking. Eleanor and I can just say it wouldn't do us any good. What's your excuse?"

"I'm going to say I'm scared of needles, but I'm thinking about it," I said. "Dr. Davidson will probably be there, given he is Candace's plastic surgeon. If so, that will be good because I told him I was frightened. Anyway, what usually happens at Botox parties? I've heard them mentioned on TV, but that's about the extent of my knowledge."

"I made Eleanor google it," Matilda said. "What a shame Botox injections weren't around in Miss Marple's time. Otherwise, she might have some sound advice for us."

I smiled. "Yes, it's a pity, isn't it."

Matilda nodded. "Apparently, people sit around and drink alcohol and have Botox injections. To clarify, I suppose it's a party where people are injected with Botox."

"I really can't picture it," I said.

"And they probably have dermal fillers as well," Matilda added, rearranging a tray of lemon cupcakes with lavender frosting.

I wished I could think of a way to get out of the party. It didn't sound like my idea of fun.

The day passed quickly, and at six, Matilda, Eleanor and I piled into my car and headed in the direction of Candace and Rick Weatherspoon's house. Eleanor was navigating, and I was impressed. "You're a good navigator," I said to Eleanor.

"I guess I've had plenty of practice," Eleanor began, before Matilda, who was in the back seat, leaned forward and tapped Eleanor on her shoulder.

They didn't say another word until we arrived at the Weatherspoons' house. A curved driveway swept past manicured lawns and hedges. The house itself was substantial and imposing, cream brick with a red roof and several dormer windows.

Cherri met us at the door. "Oh Jane darling, I said you had to dress up," she said with obvious disappointment, looking me up and down.

My spirits fell. "I did dress up," I said, looking down at my pretty dress.

"You look good," Matilda whispered in my ear, "not like those others."

It did seem to me that everyone was dressed in an over the top manner. They looked as though they were going to a significant event, not a private party in someone's home. Cherri, for one, was wearing a tight, low-cut, green dress which appeared to be comprised wholly of oversized sequins.

Candace, dressed in soft pink ruffles, hurried over and took my hand with both her hands. "It's lovely to see you again, Jane. Thankfully it's under better circumstances this time."

I introduced Matilda and Eleanor. Candace nodded at them and promptly left.

"Now see what you can find out," Cherri said in a whisper.

The champagne was flowing freely. A waiter came over and pushed a champagne flute into my hands. "No thanks, I'm driving," I said. She smiled and hurried away. I placed the flute on an elegant table.

The foyer had a spectacular marble in various shades of gray and my eye was drawn to two giant bronze statues standing in front of the curved staircase. Cherri led us into another room. This room was expansive, although the ceiling height seemed a little lower than it should have been in such a house as this. Here the carpets were cream and walls buttercup yellow. From this room could be seen various other rooms, such as a billiards room and a sitting room. Multi-colored floor rugs were scattered everywhere. The furniture was white but adorned with cushions of every color.

"Jane," a voice said behind me. I turned around to see Melissa Matheson. "I'm so sorry about your husband," I said.

"Candace insisted I come here tonight," she said. "She's worried about leaving me alone."

I introduced Matilda and Eleanor, and then Matilda said, "So you haven't returned to New York?"

Melissa shook her head. "No, the police said I have to stay in town after, you know, after what happened to Marcus."

We all offered our condolences.

Candace returned and handed each of us a sheet of paper. "What is it?" I asked Cherri.

"It's a legal waiver of course," she said. "It

absolves the doctor and nurse of responsibility if something goes wrong."

"I see," I said. "Well, I'm not going to have any."

Cherri was visibly surprised. "But, but it's a Botox party," she stammered.

"Yes, but we both know why I'm here, don't we?" When she simply looked at me blankly, I wiggled my eyebrows. Finally, she clutched her throat and laughed. "Oh yes, I see. Of course! But shouldn't you just pretend?"

"How can someone pretend to be injected with Botox?" I asked her.

She looked confused and sipped her champagne daintily.

Dr. Davidson was soon ushered into the room with a woman who was announced as Julia, the nurse. Candace hurried over to welcome them.

Dr. Davidson caught sight of me. "I didn't expect to see you here. Have you changed your mind?"

"I'm not quite there yet," I said. "I thought it would be good for me to see it happen to other people and that might make me more confident."

"Yes, that's a very good idea," he said. His tone was genuine. He smiled and excused himself.

A moment of panic hit me when I realized I had previously told him that Candace Weatherspoon recommended him. I certainly hoped he wouldn't bring it up with her, but I didn't see why he would bother.

As Candace was still standing next to me, I took the opportunity to question her. "Candace, can only a doctor administer Botox and dermal fillers in this state?"

Eleanor had already done an internet search of course, although the information was somewhat confusing.

"A nurse can administer it under the supervision of a doctor," she said. "Julia always comes here with Dr. Davidson, but he goes out and spends time with Rick. They're good friends, and this is a girls only party you see."

"Yes that makes sense," I said, at the same time thinking that it sounded awfully irresponsible to me when the law stated he should supervise.

Candace moved away to speak with someone else, and I noticed that some of the women were standing around giggling. A woman I didn't know staggered over to me, clutching a glass. She reeked of gin. "I'm only going to have a tiny bit between my eyebrows," she said, pointing to the location in question. I peered at her face.

"But surely you don't need it," I said.

She laughed. "You're so kind." However, I meant it. Her skin was stretched so tightly that a tennis ball would bounce off it freely. She didn't have so much as a single fine line.

Candace and Melissa walked arm in arm past me. "You really should have some more fillers," Candace said to Melissa. "It will cheer you up."

"I suppose you're right," she said, "but it doesn't seem the right thing to do now with Marcus gone." She sniffled.

Matilda took me aside. We stood under the cover of a giant Japanese Peace Lily. "You know, these people are getting more and more inebriated. Dr. Davidson is with Candace's husband in the pool house, so keep an eye on those vials of Botox. Cherri tells me Candace has Botox parties on a regular basis."

"Yes, but it's important to note that Candace's husband, Rick, and Dr. Davidson are good friends," I said. "That would make it very easy for Rick to procure all the Botox he needed from the doctor."

Matilda disagreed. "The doctor would have to be in on it, in that case."

I bit my lip. I didn't think of that. After an interval, I added, "But you have to admit it, Rick has better access to Botox than a normal person would have."

"Yes, but Melissa and Candace have the best access," Matilda said. "And Cherri too, for that matter."

Julia, the nurse, came over and introduced herself. She seemed quite a pleasant woman. However, she did her best to encourage us to have Botox. "You only have to spend fifty dollars," she encouraged us.

"We're past it," Eleanor said. "There's not enough Botox in the world to help us." She gestured to Matilda and herself.

"You're never too old," Julia said smoothly.

"We've only come here for the free alcohol," Matilda said, and I did my best not to laugh.

Julia turned her attention to me. "What about you? You could certainly do with Botox and dermal fillers. It would make such a difference to you, I guarantee you. If you let me inject you, you won't recognize yourself when you look in the mirror."

I had no doubt her words were true. "I'm thinking it over," I said, and then sent up a silent prayer for forgiveness for my barefaced lie. "Besides,

I was in Dr. Davidson's clinic yesterday discussing it with him, and I told him I have to pluck up the courage first."

Julia nodded slowly. "I see. What if I just give you a tiny little bit and you can see how you feel?"

"No, thanks for the kind offer, but I'll watch other people have it."

"Look, if you're scared of needles, you can lay down on the couch," she said. "If you lie down, you won't be so afraid."

"No, I'm sorry. I don't think that would help me," I said.

A look of barely concealed annoyance passed over Julia's face. "All right. If you have any questions, I'm happy to answer them for you."

I thanked her.

Matilda, Eleanor, and I sat next to each other on a large couch that afforded a good view of the room. "Should that bleed so freely?" I whispered to Matilda when Julia spent a lot of time wiping someone's face.

"Alcohol thins the blood," Eleanor said, "and that lady has had considerably more to drink than everyone else."

"You're awfully observant," I said to Eleanor.

For some reason, she didn't look pleased with the compliment.

The ladies who had already had the Botox were taking selfies and posting them somewhere, I assume to Facebook and Instagram.

It was rather boring sitting there watching all the women have injections. I wasn't at all squeamish, because I had administered first aid to horses and cattle before and had even assisted mares foaling when the foals were malpresented. As I sat there thoroughly bored, I tried to think up questions I could ask both Melissa and Candace but came up blank.

When I complained of this to Matilda, she said, "You don't need to question anyone. If the opportunity presents itself, well that's well and good, but we're here to keep an eye on those Botox vials. And from what I've seen so far, it would be quite easy to get one."

I looked at the women. Everyone was sitting around chatting happily. They had clearly had too much to drink, apart from Julia, who was concentrating on her current patient. The vials of Botox and dermal fillers sat on a little table. "Anyone could walk past and pinch one and no one would notice," I said to Matilda.

She stood up. "I'll try," she said.

Matilda walked across the room. In one smooth move, she picked up a vial, put it in her skirt pocket, and then glided over the other side to the bar.

I was shocked. "That means anyone could do it," I said to Eleanor. "If the Botox parties are always like this, then anyone could have stolen it."

"Oh no, Matilda is a professional," Eleanor said.

I was shocked. "What? Are you saying Matilda is a professional thief?"

Eleanor's hand flew to her throat. "Oh no, of course, I didn't mean that. I just meant Matilda is professionally sneaky." She laughed. "What an imagination you have, Jane."

I laughed too. I watched as Matilda swept back and put the little vial back on the table. Even though I had been watching her and waiting for her to do it, I could scarcely see her do it.

"Anyone could take one," Matilda said upon her return. "Why don't you have a turn, Jane?"

"No way!" I said. "There's no way I'm going to pinch a bottle of Botox."

"But you are to put it straight back again, of course," Matilda said.

"What if someone sees me?" I said. I held up

both hands, palms outwards, in protest. "There's no way I'm going to do it."

Matilda looked crestfallen. "It's quite fun, really. Well then, since it's so freely available, it could have been Melissa or Candace."

"And Cherri," Eleanor pointed out.

"But Julia would have noticed a vial of Botox missing afterwards," I pointed out.

"Not necessarily," Matilda said. "Someone could have taken a few half used vials and substituted them with vials of purified water. Julia would never know the difference."

Eleanor agreed.

"It's a good time to question the suspects now that they've had a bit too much to drink," Matilda said to me. "Look, here comes Melissa."

I stood up. "Oh Melissa, your face looks so different," I said honestly.

"Thank you," she said. I figured she was attempting to smile, although nothing moved.

"I hope it has cheered you up a little, if that's even possible?" I continued.

"Yes a little," she said.

"I was hoping to speak with you at some time because I want to ask you a question about Ted."

"Ted?" she said. Her tone sounded surprised yet once again her expression remained impassive.

"Yes. It's a little embarrassing. You know, I was married to Ted for some years, but Cherri has told me recently that Ted did something untoward, something I didn't know about."

She did not speak, so I continued, "Would you have any idea what it could be?"

"Do you mean like a guilty secret?"

"Yes, that's exactly what I mean," I said, nodding as I spoke. "Cherri doesn't know of any guilty secret. What's more, I was married to Ted for a long time and I don't know of one either. Would you happen to know if Ted is hiding a guilty secret?"

To my great surprise, she said, "Yes."

CHAPTER 12

I awoke the next morning quite disappointed. I had tossed and turned all night as I had not managed to find out Ted's secret from Melissa. What's more, I was surprised that Melissa knew what it was, whereas I had been married to Ted for all those years and didn't have a clue. I had asked her what the secret was, but she had said she felt sick and had left early. That meant I would have to seek her out, and that could become quite uncomfortable. It's a shame it hadn't happened naturally.

As I staggered out to the kitchen to make coffee, Mr. Crumbles ran in front of my legs, almost tripping me.

"He's just hungry," Eleanor said. "I slept in." She poured some food into his bowl.

Matilda burst out of her bedroom, pen and paper in hand. "I didn't sleep in! I've been hard at work coming up with a plan," she announced proudly.

My stomach sank. "What will you try to get me into now?" I said sadly.

She shook her finger at me. "On the contrary, it is *I* who will be in the firing line. I have come up with a foolproof plan. I'm going to invite Ted to a local café and give him the third degree."

"But why would he speak to you?" I asked her.

"I haven't finished yet," she said, rolling her eyes. "I'm going in disguise as a private detective. Maybe I'll even wear a deer stalker hat and smoke a pipe just like Sherlock Marple." She laughed after she said it, but I wasn't so sure she was joking.

"So, are we still going to stick to the story that Cherri hired a private investigator?

She shook her head. "No, I had a conversation with Cherri last night and she told me she doesn't have money, not her own anyway. She couldn't afford to hire a private detective."

"Then what will you say to Ted?" I was perplexed.

"Never you mind." Matilda's tone was smug. "I can't tell you now because that will ruin the flow of my creative genius, but I have it all figured out. I will tell you this much—I'm going to book two tables at the café."

"Two tables?" Eleanor looked up from stroking Mr. Crumbles. "Why two tables?"

"Because I'm going to sit at one table, and you and Jane are going to sit at the adjoining table and listen in to the conversation."

"Won't Ted think it strange that I'm there?" I said, raising my eyebrows.

Matilda chuckled. "No, you're going to have your back to him and you'll be wearing Amish clothes."

I held up both hands in protest. "No way! Not again! There's no way I'm doing that!"

"It's the only way, don't you see?"

"No."

"This is my plan. I know this particular café well. It has booths, not the short sort of booths but the long ones. At one section they back directly onto each other with only a framework between the seats that runs up the wall. I'll make sure Ted sits on the one adjoining the other seat and you and Eleanor can sit directly behind him listening into everything he says. That way if I miss something, you can hear it."

"Shouldn't we plant a bugging device on him?" Eleanor said seriously. "That would be much easier than making Jane go in disguise as Amish again."

"That had occurred to me," Matilda said, nodding and smiling as she spoke, "but our last bugging device broke. I'm sure we can manage without one."

"You had a bugging device?" I asked her in shock.

"Never you mind, Jane," Matilda said. "I know Rebecca keeps a spare change of clothes in the back room, so you can simply wear those. Your back will be to Ted and he'll never know it's you." She waved a bunch of papers at me. "I've written it all out. You and Eleanor will get there half an hour early to make sure your backs are to him. I will insist he sits with his back to you."

"But what if he doesn't?" I said, thinking the plan quite silly.

"Leave it to Matilda," Eleanor said. "She knows what she's doing."

This was getting stranger and stranger. "I suppose so," I said. I didn't like to admit it, but I found our expeditions somewhat exciting. They gave me an adrenaline rush. It was the most exciting thing I had done all my life. "Rebecca won't like it," I added.

"Well, don't tell her," Matilda said. "I'm sure she won't ask you so you won't have to lie."

I bit the end of one fingernail. "What are you going to ask him?"

"I'm going to interrogate him about his secret," she said.

My stomach was churning all morning until it was time to leave for lunch. As it was a Saturday, we always shut at twelve. I changed into the Amish clothes and then the horrible realization that Matilda would have to drive struck me.

"Drive slowly, won't you," I pleaded, and then was flung back in my seat as she hit the gas.

I thought it was easier for me to sit with my hands over my eyes. I was relieved when the car came to a stop. "Now run along, Jane and Eleanor. You have to make sure Ted doesn't see you."

"What are we going to do for half an hour?" I asked her.

"Drink coffee. Eat cake. You're at a café."

There was no suitable response.

The restaurant was quite pretty in an unusual sort of way. The booths were heavily upholstered in a dark velvet floral fabric. Large abstract pictures hung from the walls. The front section had five booths, each of them separated by a grid over which was growing luscious ivy. The booths opened up onto a more typical café seating. Potted plants adorned the whole room. A delightful fragrance of jasmine permeated the room and I suspected scented candles were nearby.

We were shown to our table and at once I could see the wisdom of Matilda's plan. I sat with my back directly behind where Ted would be sitting. There was only a short distance between the two booths that backed onto each other. The framework covered with the ivy provided a good visual yet not audio barrier.

Ted had never seen Matilda or Eleanor, so he wouldn't be the least suspicious. I pushed my hair back up into my prayer *kapp* and pulled my bonnet over my face, although there was no need. Melissa had been right; Ted would be unable to see my face.

Eleanor and I both ordered coffee and Shoo-fly pie and waited for Ted to arrive. Eleanor's phone rang directly after we ordered. "It's Matilda," she told me. She answered the phone and nodded a few times before hanging up. "Matilda said she's coming into the café now so she can sit in the correct place, and then Ted will be forced to sit directly behind you. She says you're not to speak from now on. If you want any food, point to the menu and I'll order it for you." I nodded.

Eleanor pushed on. "We are not to look at Matilda. We're to stay here until they both leave and then she'll call us and tell us when the coast is clear." She looked at me expectantly, so I nodded again.

"And Jane, it's essential you don't speak at all, because Ted will recognize your voice and the game will be up."

I pulled a face and nodded. I wasn't quite the sleuth that Matilda and Eleanor were, but I had figured that much for myself.

Only a few minutes later, Eleanor kicked me under the table. I translated that to mean that Matilda was coming. I assume she took up her position in the booth.

About five minutes later, Eleanor kicked me again. I translated that to mean Ted was coming into view. Suddenly, my palms were sweaty and I wiped them on my overskirt.

Ted wasted no time coming to the point, and I

was pleased I could hear him clearly. "Miss Marple, I don't understand why you summoned me and said it was so urgent."

I tried not to chuckle at Matilda's false name.

"I'm a private detective," Matilda told him. "You're a person of interest to the police because they believe the vic was blackmailing you over a previous incident."

If Ted was surprised, his voice showed no sign. "Well, I'm certainly not going to employ you, if that's what you're hoping."

"Not at all," Matilda said, her voice steely. "Your wife, Cherri, hired my services."

Now Ted was surprised. "Cherri?" he said in a high-pitched voice. "But she doesn't have her own money."

"It's pro bono," Matilda said in an officious tone. "Here in Lancaster, we do pro bono services for people without money."

"But Cherri is wealthy," Ted protested.

"You just said she didn't have any of her own money," Matilda said.

Ted made a strangled sound back of his throat. "But she can use my money."

"Then would you pay my bill?" Matilda said.

"No," Ted sputtered.

"Then that's settled," Matilda said. "I hope you'll accept my help. Your wife will be most upset if you don't."

"Why didn't she tell me?" Ted said.

"She wanted it to be a surprise," Matilda said.

"It is!" Ted spat.

"Look, do you want my help or not? I'm a highly experienced investigator."

There was a long silence, and I could imagine Ted storming out of the café. I was surprised when he said, "Go on. I don't want to upset my wife."

Eleanor and I smiled at each other. Just then the waiter approached. "Would you like to order anything else?" he asked me.

I nodded and pointed to my empty coffee cup. I kicked Eleanor under the table, but she just sat there.

The waiter didn't take the hint, either. "What would you like?" he said.

I kicked Eleanor harder and pointed to my empty coffee cup again. "Oh, she wants another coffee, I think?" Eleanor said, and I nodded.

"And what did you think of the Shoo-fly pie?" the waiter asked me. "I always ask Amish customers what they think of the Shoo-fly pie."

I smiled widely and gave him the thumbs up, but he looked puzzled and continued to stare at me.

Apparently, it was all getting too much for Eleanor. "She has taken a vow of silence," Eleanor said.

"A vow of silence?" the waiter said. He looked thoroughly confused now.

"Yes, she's one of those Amish sects that take the vow of silence," Eleanor said, ignoring me frowning deeply at her.

"I thought that was only Catholic monks."

Eleanor shook her head.

"But she spoke before," the waiter said.

Eleanor put her finger to her lips. "Yes, and I have rebuked her thoroughly. Please don't tell her bishop should he come in for coffee."

The waiter picked up our empty coffee cups. "No I won't," he said before he left.

I glared and wiggled my eyebrows at Eleanor, but she simply shrugged.

We had missed a whole slab of what Ted was saying. I listened in once more.

Matilda was speaking. "Mr. Delight, I can't help you if you're not perfectly honest with me."

"But you'll tell my wife, since she's the one who engaged your services," Ted pointed out.

"Well, if it's something that bad, perhaps you yourself should be telling your wife anyway," Matilda said. "If the police keep pushing this line of inquiry, then it will become public. Do you want that?"

"No, I suppose not," Ted said in a resigned manner.

"Then what could you have possibly done to warrant blackmail?"

Ted let out a long sigh. I held my breath, wanting to hear his secret. "I have a brother," Ted said, "but he's since gone to live somewhere in Africa." He stopped speaking.

"Go on," Matilda prompted him.

"We didn't get on at all well and I haven't seen him in many years. Anyway, I was caught with recreational drugs. The police arrested and charged me. I gave my brother's name when I was arrested."

I gasped and then covered it with a cough.

"Do go on," Matilda said.

"I couldn't have been a lawyer with a previous conviction for possession of drugs," Ted said, "so that's why I gave my brother's name. To clarify, I *could* have been a lawyer, but I would have had to disclose the previous conviction to the bar association. I didn't want to do that. It would have made it hard for me, very hard."

"I understand that, but how did your brother react?"

Ted chuckled. "Not well at all, not at first. Still, he was never interested in law so I paid him a handsome sum of money to take the rap for me. There was no jail time or anything, just a criminal record. Even though I gave him a large sum of money, we had a falling out. That was the last I saw him. I was quite young at the time."

"So your brother has a previous conviction, but you don't right?" Matilda said. "This is the secret?"

"Yes, and it might not sound such a bad secret to you…" Ted began, but Matilda interrupted him.

"Actually, it does sound like a serious matter."

"No matter." I could picture Ted waving his hand at Matilda to dismiss her words.

"And the police are aware of this? The police believe the vic was blackmailing you."

"I believe so," he said, "only Marcus wasn't blackmailing me."

"Did Marcus actually know that your brother has a previous conviction instead of you?" Matilda asked him.

Ted said, "I've known Marcus for ages. He and

my brother were good friends years ago. Perhaps my brother got drunk and told him, but Marcus never mentioned it to me."

"Are you absolutely certain of that?" Matilda asked him.

"Yes, Marcus never mentioned a word of it to me. I don't know how word got out, so I can only assume that my brother told Marcus at one point and Marcus told his wife."

"So do you think Melissa Matheson is trying to frame you for her husband's murder?"

"Not frame as such, but she might genuinely think I did it," Ted said. "She's very good friends with Candace Weatherspoon. She wouldn't want to think Candace or Rick did it and she wouldn't like to think it was the staff, so she has to blame someone. I'm the only one left she can blame."

I could hear Matilda's fingers drumming on the table. "Let me get this straight. Your brother told Marcus who told Melissa about the previous conviction. You think Melissa is looking for someone to blame, and that person is you."

"Yes, what else could it be?" Ted asked in a belligerent manner. "So how can you help me?"

"I have to go back to my office and consult my

notes," Matilda said. I heard a shuffling sound and knew she was standing up.

"May I have one of your business cards?" Ted asked her.

Matilda said, "No."

It was all I could do not to laugh.

CHAPTER 13

I was driving Rebecca, Matilda, and Eleanor to a barn raising. We had been discussing Ted.

"I'm surprised you didn't know Ted's brother?" Matilda said.

"Yes, like I said before, I never met him. He didn't even come to our wedding."

Rebecca spoke up. "Thanks for driving me, Jane."

I looked across at Rebecca in the passenger seat. "You're welcome. Are you sure this is a good idea?"

She nodded. "I couldn't sit at home alone with everyone else working so hard. It just wouldn't be right. Surely there's something I can do with my left hand. I'd be able to carry a plate of food at least."

Rebecca's husband, Ephraim, had been there all day helping the men, and Rebecca normally would have been at the farm all day baking for the workers, but for her broken arm.

I smiled. The Amish were amazing at helping each other out. The Rocke family's barn had been old and past repair, so the whole community had come together to raise a new barn. Of course, all the labour was free, and the community had also donated all the materials. It wasn't a particularly large barn and the wooden frame structure was going up in one day. Of course, the preparations had been done well in advance. It was the first time I had been to a barn raising in decades.

The Amish women always gathered to make big meals for the men who were working awfully hard.

As we approached the Rocke family's farm, I could see that the frame was already half built. We drove on past row after row of horses and buggies, the horses tied to rails.

"I've noticed it before but I never thought to ask," Eleanor said. "Why are all the buggies dark? I suppose you couldn't paint one red with yellow zigzags, for example?"

Rebecca laughed, as did I. I imagined if Eleanor had ever been Amish, she most certainly would drive a buggy painted red with yellow zigzags.

"The buggies in our community are gray-topped buggies," Rebecca told her. "The Ordnung determines what color the buggies can be."

I knew I didn't need to explain the Ordnung to Matilda and Eleanor. They had been around Rebecca long enough to know the Ordnung was the unwritten set of rules for each community. Despite popular belief, one Amish community differed in many ways from another. What was right for one community might not be right for another.

"I've seen bright yellow buggies though," Eleanor continued.

Rebecca nodded. "The Byler Amish drive those buggies. They're an Old Order community."

I parked out front and ran around to help Rebecca out of the car. "The doctor said you're supposed to rest," I scolded her.

"*Nee*, I'm fine," she said as she walked away. I sighed. Nothing came between an Amish person and their work.

I walked in the kitchen to see a flurry of activity. Some of the ladies were rolling pastry, while others were busy making sandwiches. Everyone was chatting happily, but everything was working with precision. The smell of good Amish coffee permeated the air.

Wanda Hershberger was the first to greet us. "*Hiya*, Jane, Matilda, and Eleanor. What are you doing here, Rebecca? You should be at home, resting."

"I can do something," Rebecca protested. "I can stir something, surely. Would somebody give me some eggs to beat?"

Someone immediately appeared with a whisk and soon Rebecca was beating eggs with her left hand—don't ask me how she did it—and I was left to admire the way the Amish women got everything done and at that, without electricity. These days I took electricity for granted, but there had been a time when I had to do without it. I particularly remembered having to pull the cord to start the diesel motor on the old Maytag wringer washer. It was a laborious process, putting the clothes through the wringer into the rinsing tub, rinsing them and then putting them through the wringer again.

I shook my head. As much as I envied the Amish, their sense of community and their work ethic, there was no way I could ever return.

"Is there anything we can do to help?" I asked Wanda.

"Would you make some funeral pies?"

"Sure." I turned to Eleanor and Matilda. "I'll show you how to make funeral pies."

Eleanor raised her eyebrows. "But no one has died." The Amish ladies standing by all chuckled.

"You could call it a raisin pie," I told her. "It got the name *Funeral Pie* because people took these pies to the family of someone who had passed away. As you know, Amish these days have gas refrigerators, but in the days before refrigeration, even if fresh fruit wasn't available, most homes had dried raisins. The ingredients are always available and the pie keeps for ages. People could make it a couple days before the funeral, and it doesn't need refrigeration. You can freeze it for up to three months," I told them.

"So it's a raisin pie, you say?" Matilda asked me.

I nodded. "It has raisins obviously, as well as cornstarch, sugar, brown sugar, cinnamon, allspice, apple cider vinegar and butter. We always used water, but some families use milk. Basically, it's a double crusted pie with a lattice top. It tastes quite nice. I'm probably not describing it too well. I'll make one when we go home tonight."

"You have enough to do. Maybe you can bake one after this business has all blown over," Matilda said, wriggling her eyebrows in what I figured was her way of saying I could make one after the murder was solved.

I combined the sugar, brown sugar, cornstarch, salt and spices in a bowl and stirred, while Matilda made the dough. Wanda Hershberger came over and introduced us to her daughter. "I've always talked about Waneta—well, here she is!"

We all greeted each other warmly.

"Thanks so much for the information," I added.

She smiled. "I probably shouldn't be passing it on."

"We're all grateful that you do," Matilda said. She lowered her voice and said, "Have the toxicology results come back yet? Clostridium botulinum?"

When Waneta nodded, Matilda said, "Everyone expected that, but now this is confirmation."

Waneta turned back to her baking. Eleanor was making sandwiches as we were speaking. I was impressed that her speed could almost match the Amish ladies. I added water to the raisins and then heated and stirred until the mixture started to bubble.

"It's almost time to feed the *menner* now," someone said, and everyone at once clutched a tray of sandwiches or a pie. I set the mixture aside to cool and grabbed a plate of sandwiches.

"It's way past lunchtime," Eleanor said.

"They don't feed the men just lunch, dinner, and breakfast," I told her. "They need to eat. They have small meals throughout the day to keep up their strength. They're doing hard physical labour."

We walked outside to low rows of wooden tables and chairs. Some of the men were already sitting and others were coming in from the wooden frame. I knew those table and benches were for the church gatherings, which they called 'meetings,' every second Sunday. The Amish did not have a building in which to worship. Instead, they alternated meetings at people's houses. During a meeting, the men always sat on one side of the room, and the women on the other, but if the house was too small, the men and women sat in separate rooms with the preacher walking between the rooms. Sometimes the meetings were held in barns.

Memories of my youth flooded back. The meetings generally lasted three hours. There were two sermons, the shorter first and lasting about twenty minutes, and the second lasting about an hour. Hymns were sung from the Ausbund, the Amish hymn book, and always without musical instruments. It wasn't until I left the Amish that I realized just how slowly the hymns were sung.

The tables and chairs set out for the men were used for the meetings. Rather, the chairs were used for the meetings and then the tables were brought out for the big meals that followed the meetings.

I set my plate of sandwiches down and went back for more, keeping an eye on Rebecca. She seemed to be managing all right carrying one pie in her hand, but I was worried, as she should be resting.

There was a flurry of activity for a while until all the men were eating happily.

"What happens now?" Eleanor asked me.

"Everyone keeps baking and preparing for dinner, and then they wait until the men have finished and clean up after them."

"Oh, and they don't have dishwashers," Matilda said, clutching her throat in alarm.

I laughed.

"Do you mind if we leave?" Eleanor said. "I'm a little worried about leaving Mr. Crumbles by himself for so long. He doesn't like to be alone."

We said our goodbyes to Rebecca and the other ladies and were already halfway to my car when

Waneta called to us. I turned around and hurried back to her, followed by Matilda and Eleanor.

Waneta looked around and then said in little more than a whisper, "There's some information from the medical examiner's office. I don't know if I should tell you, but it's not a secret as such. The police have been freely talking about it."

"What is it?" I prompted her.

"The victim's wife, Melissa Matheson, took out a life insurance policy on her husband."

"Did she now?" I said.

"But that's not so uncommon," Eleanor pointed out.

"It is if it was taken out not long before he was murdered," Matilda said.

"How much was he insured for?" I asked Waneta.

"Five million dollars."

CHAPTER 14

.

"That's it!" Matilda said as we drove away. "I'm going to question Melissa Matheson right now."

"Could you pretend you're an insurance investigator?" Eleanor asked.

Matilda appeared to be thinking it over. "Actually, that's not a bad idea, but I think it's best if I keep my cover as the private investigator. If I tell Melissa that Cherri sent me there to speak with her, she can hardly refuse to see me. I might get more out of her that way."

"I wish we could be there too," Eleanor said wistfully.

"I know, I'll go and buy some audio spy

equipment so both of you can sit outside her house in the car and hear what I'm saying."

"If only I could," Eleanor said wistfully, "but I need to spend some quality time with Mr. Crumbles."

"Why don't you bring him?" Matilda said.

"What a good idea!" Eleanor sounded quite cheery. "I'm sure he'd love to go for a ride in the car. All he gets to see are walls of the apartment and the courtyard outside. You know, I'm thinking of training him to walk on a leash."

I didn't think taking Mr. Crumbles was such a good idea, but I wasn't going to say. After all, trouble seemed to follow Mr. Crumbles. Visions of how my behind sticking out that dog door must have looked to others flashed through my mind. I shuddered and tried to think of something else.

"Jane can drive to a surveillance store after we collect Mr. Crumbles," Matilda announced.

"I don't know where one is," I said, taking one hand off the wheel to scratch my head.

"I can direct you."

I shot a glance across at Eleanor. How did she know where a surveillance shop was?

"We'll go home and collect Mr. Crumbles first,"

Eleanor said. "And we need to give Cherri the heads up."

Before I even had a chance to respond, my cell phone rang. My car was too old to have Bluetooth, so I indicated to Matilda that she should answer the phone.

"Hi Cherri, Jane is driving. I'll put you on speaker so everyone can hear."

There were strange sounds on the phone and at first I thought it was a bad connection until I realized Cherri was sobbing.

"What's wrong?" I asked in a loud voice.

Matilda at once held the phone close to me.

"The police have questioned Ted again," she wailed. "Are you close to solving the murder?"

"Actually we were just about to call you," I told her. "We want to question Melissa Matheson now. Actually, Matilda is going to question her and pretend she's a private investigator working for you. Is that all right with you?"

Cherri sniffled before answering. "Of course. Anything you want to do is fine with me. Jane darling, did you find out anything from Ted?"

"I'll tell you about that later," I said, trying to avoid the question. After all, I wanted to break the news to her in person. And I was hoping Ted himself would tell her. After thinking things through for a few moments, I said to Cherri, "We'll call you after Matilda questions Melissa and decides on a time to meet."

Cherri thanked me and hung up. "I feel sorry for her," I said.

"Honestly, Jane, she was having an affair with your husband, you didn't even know, and then she had his baby. It must be your Amish upbringing that's making you so kind hearted."

I laughed. "Don't you feel sorry for her too? It's not as if I have any feelings for Ted anymore. Not nice ones, anyway." I scowled. "I'm sure he took advantage of her."

"That's all well and good, but what if she's the murderer?" Eleanor piped up from the back seat.

"Why would she want to murder Marcus?" I asked her.

"Who would know? We have to investigate to find out," Eleanor said reasonably.

"Maybe she and Melissa are in it together," Matilda pointed out. "In Agatha Christie movies, sometimes the murderer has an accomplice."

We had arrived home. It wasn't long before Eleanor had collected Mr. Crumbles and we were all back in the car.

I picked up the conversation where we had left off. "What possible reason would Cherri have to help Melissa murder Marcus?" I said, thinking this was all a little far-fetched.

"I know, it's the old swapping murders device," Matilda said rather happily. "I saw it on *Death in Paradise* once. Maybe Cherri murdered Marcus and Melissa will murder Ted."

"It sounds a bit unbelievable to me," I said.

"You'd be surprised," Matilda said. "I'll be interested to see if Cherri has a life insurance policy on Ted."

"But even Ted told you that Cherri has no money of her own."

"But maybe she talked Ted into it."

To my relief, Mr. Crumbles did not appear to mind being in the car. He sat on Eleanor's lap and put his paws on the window staring outside. "He's having a good time," Eleanor said, followed by, "Oh no!"

"What happened?" I asked her.

"His bowl of water splashed in your car. Sorry, Jane. Maybe I filled it a little too full. Oh well, it's not full now."

Eleanor had insisted on bringing Mr. Crumbles' water bowl, food bowl, and even his litter tray. One small mercy was that his litter tray was one of those enclosed ones with a carbon filter at the top and a swinging door. Still, I was sure some litter crystals would manage to find their way onto my car floor.

Matilda leaned over the back seat and scowled at Eleanor. "It's a wonder you didn't bring the pole for him."

Eleanor muttered something under her breath.

There was no more chance for conversation, or bickering, because we had arrived at the surveillance store.

Eleanor stayed in the car with Mr. Crumbles, while Matilda and I went inside to buy an audio recorder.

The young man serving shot us a dubious look. "Can I help you ladies?"

"Yes, we're looking for an audio spy device that's well concealed and accurate," Matilda said. "I don't know too much about the modern versions."

"Oh, are you wishing to record a business meeting?" he asked.

"Does it matter what we need to record?" Matilda said. "We want a professional quality audio spy device, that's all. We don't need a long battery life with it, but it needs to be concealed nicely."

"We do have several voice recorders that can

fit in a purse or pocket. We also have pens and USB memory sticks. Our pens will actually write. We also have keychain digital voice audio recorders."

"No, I'm not keen on memory sticks or pens," Matilda told him. "I want something more substantial. And what's more, we need it to feedback to people listening within four hundred yards."

Now the man really was surprised. "So you want someone to be able to listen in real time? You don't simply want a recording?"

"Yes, exactly," Matilda said. "We're looking for a transmitter as well as a recorder. You know, like a police wire."

"I see," he said, nodding slowly as he spoke. "We don't get much call for that."

"Do you have any at all?"

"Yes, we do. I'll show you our models."

I could see at once that Matilda was not happy with the selection.

"Is the recording in person or over a phone?" the shop assistant asked.

"In person," she said. "We only need to record up to an hour. But as I said, we do want other people to be able to hear it at the time."

He handed her a USB stick. "This will give you fifteen hours of recording on a single charge."

Matilda looked it over. "Do you have anything more substantial?"

"Most people want to record phone conversations," he said, "but this one is voice-activated and it has a lot of battery power. The audio is very clear. It's larger than the pen or the USB flash drive audio recorder, but you can conceal it in your purse."

Matilda took some time deciding, but finally said, "I'll have that one."

I opened my purse, but she said, "No Jane, allow me."

"But I feel responsible because Cherri asked for my help," I said.

Matilda pulled a face. "Nonsense. Besides, it's wonderful to have a surveillance device again."

I wondered why she said 'again', but she was already paying for the device.

When we got back to the car, Eleanor asked, "What one did you get?"

Matilda handed it over to her. After a few moments, Eleanor said, "This is not good at all."

"What do you expect from one that's available to the general public?" Matilda said, mystifying me even more. I would love to know what these ladies had been up to in the past.

"Now hand it back Eleanor, so I can set it up," Matilda ordered her. "Find Melissa Matheson's address on the GPS on your phone so you can navigate for Jane."

"What did you think I was doing when you were buying the voice recorder?" Eleanor said. "And Jane, Cherri called while you were in there. I saw the Caller ID, so I answered. I hope you don't mind."

"No, I'm glad you did," I said.

"Cherri is going to set up an appointment for Matilda to speak with Melissa now."

"Excellent." Matilda looked across at me. "Jane, put these on!" She handed me a prayer *kapp* and bonnet. "Melissa knows what you look like, so you'll need to wear these."

I tapped myself on my forehead. "But Matilda, I completely forgot! How could I have forgotten? Melissa knows what you look like too. You were at the Botox party with me."

"That's perfectly fine," she said. "She already thinks that Cherri has engaged my services. I'll just tell her I was there undercover. If you will recall, we were never introduced as your roommates."

"I can't remember. You have such a good memory, Matilda. Anyway, what if Melissa sees Eleanor in the car?"

"I wouldn't worry about that," Matilda said, "and your disguise is simply a precaution. Your windows are tinted. By the way, when you park out front, don't do so directly outside the door. Try to park under some sort of cover."

Melissa's house was even bigger than the Weatherspoons' house. Large and sprawling, it stood behind imposing electronic gates. We had to announce ourselves into the intercom and then the gates opened for us.

"Gosh, I'm glad they don't have guard dogs because Mr. Crumbles might be scared if they run up to the car," Eleanor said.

When we reached the front of the building. I parked behind a potted spicebush. It would provide minimal cover, but it was better than nothing.

As Matilda walked over to the door, I clutched my stomach. "I hope this goes well," I said to Eleanor. I adjusted my prayer *kapp* and took off my seatbelt in an attempt to make myself comfortable. Eleanor handed me the device, which looked like a small black box. "Put it up there," she said, pointing to the dash, "so we can both hear. Switch it on now."

I switched on the device, which thankfully appeared quite uncomplicated, and set it on the dash.

At first the voices were muffled and then we clearly heard Melissa's voice. "Hello, don't I know you from somewhere?"

"Yes I'm Miss Marple," Matilda said, once more giving her false name. "I'm the private investigator hired by Cherri Delight. I was at Candace Weatherspoon's Botox party the other night, working undercover."

"Oh." Melissa sounded surprised. "Did you find out anything?"

"I'm not at liberty to divulge that, I'm afraid," Matilda said.

After a few moments, Melissa spoke again. "Won't you come in?"

There was no sound for a few minutes, and then Matilda asked, "Do you know anyone who would have any reason to harm your husband?"

"I don't know who could have murdered him," she said with a sigh. "The police have already asked me this several times."

"If you wouldn't mind going through it again

with me," Matilda said. "The police don't share information with me, so I have to conduct a separate investigation."

Melissa replied at once. "Of course, of course. I do understand."

Just then, I jumped as two dog's paws landed hard on the car window. The owner of the paws was a large and angry Doberman. Bits of saliva flew out of the side of his mouth.

The next thing I knew, Mr. Crumbles flung himself at the window, making deep meowing sounds. I was rather taken aback, surprised that such sounds could come from the little cat. Apparently, the dog felt the same way. Mr. Crumbles' meows increased in volume and he swiped at the glass.

The dog whimpered and ran away, his tail between his legs. Mr. Crumbles stood on the seat with his paws on the glass and meowed several times in succession.

"Did you hear that?" I heard Melissa's voice say. "It sounded like a cat."

"Shush, she can hear you," Matilda muttered.

Eleanor tapped me on the shoulder, drew her finger across her throat, and pointed to the black box on the dash.

The next thing I heard was Melissa's voice. "Sorry, did you tell me to be quiet? I know you can hear me. I'm sure I heard a sound like a very angry cat."

"No, I didn't hear a thing. Maybe it was thunder?" Matilda said.

Eleanor lunged into the front seat, grabbed the black box, and turned it off. "The noises in the car were going through to the recorder," she said. "Clearly, Matilda did not set it up properly."

"What are we going to do now?" I said. "What if Melissa was suspicious?"

Eleanor stroked Mr. Crumbles. "Did that naughty dog upset you, you poor thing?"

I saw the Doberman off in the distance cowering under the dubious cover of pink moccasin flowers. "More like Mr. Crumbles upset the poor dog."

"Anyway, we don't need to worry because Matilda recorded it." She handed me a box.

As I opened it, I exclaimed, "Donuts!"

"It's not exactly a stakeout, but it might get quite boring waiting for Matilda," Eleanor said. "I grabbed some donuts from the fridge when we went home to collect Mr. Crumbles."

I was already eating one so I couldn't speak. I nodded and gave her the thumbs up.

We had eaten the whole box of donuts before Matilda returned. "Drive off quickly," she said, when she was half-way in the car.

"Was Melissa suspicious when she heard Mr. Crumbles?" I asked her.

Matilda shook her head. "No, not at all. She really did think his meowing was thunder. I take it you didn't hear anything after that?"

"No we didn't," I said.

Matilda made a clucking sound with her tongue. "Honestly, that wasn't a very good surveillance device."

"Did you ask her about the life insurance policy?" I asked her, edging toward the gates that were opening in front of us.

"Yes, she said she took it out about ten years ago. Either she did it so long ago so suspicion would be thrown off her and she had planned this murder a long time, or she is innocent. Most people don't wait that long to murder their husbands."

"It could just be that she is quite clever," Eleanor remarked.

"Possibly," Matilda said, "but she did tell me something very interesting." Before we had a chance to ask her what it was, she pushed on. "The chef has now moved to the top of the list of suspects."

"Brendan Bowles?" I said with surprise. "Why?"

"Because he is a highly regarded chef, and Marcus was cost-cutting. He insisted on minimal staff and he wouldn't let the chef purchase quality ingredients. Marcus was trying to cut corners as much as he could, and Brendan was furious about it."

"Why didn't Brendan just leave?" I asked her.

"Well, apparently that's why your ex-husband Ted was called in," Matilda told me. "Brendan was trying to get out of the contract and Ted was called in to advise Marcus. Ted had written the contract in the first place and it was iron clad. There was no way Brendan could get out of it, but he had employed a lawyer to contest it."

"Aha! So that's why Ted came to Pennsylvania."

Matilda nodded. "And you know how chefs can be. I've watched a lot of chef shows on TV. I'd say Brendan does have a motive."

I thought it over. "What about Candace and Rick Weatherspoon? They were the partners in the business. What is their attitude toward the understaffing and the poor quality food?"

"They were on the chef's side," Matilda said, "so it was only Marcus who was holding out and he had the controlling interest in the business."

"What is Melissa's opinion of this?" I said. "She's a partner in the business too."

"She's already given Brendan the go-ahead to employ more staff and order better quality ingredients."

Eleanor snorted from the back seat. "That didn't take her long. Her husband was only murdered a few days ago."

"She said Brendan was pressing her to agree."

I shook my head. I slowed down to pass a buggy and realized I was still wearing my Amish bonnet. Whatever would the driver think? I kept my eyes firmly on the road and then removed my bonnet and prayer *kapp* with one hand. "It sounds a little too convenient to me. She handed Brendan to you on a platter, probably to throw suspicion off herself."

Matilda disagreed. "No, Jane, she was entirely reluctant to tell me about the chef. I had to drag it out of her. She certainly didn't volunteer any information."

Once more Eleanor piped up from the back

seat. "Did Melissa think Brendan murdered Marcus?"

"She didn't say so explicitly. In fact, she didn't even hint that he might have, and she said she was sure he wouldn't have done such a thing."

"But the thing is, it had to be someone who was sitting at the dinner table that night," I said, "and we are running out of options."

CHAPTER 15

atilda, Eleanor, and I were huddled under a large umbrella on a decidedly rainy day. We were standing at the graveside at the funeral of Marcus Matheson. The driving rain came at us in waves, giving a good impression of a mountain mist.

"We should have brought more umbrellas," Matilda grumbled as the three of us stood in a huddle.

"I don't know why they didn't have the service in a church and then come out here afterwards," I said.

I wiped the rain out of my eyes and peered at the gathering crowd. Most of them I didn't know, although I spied Candace and Rick Weatherspoon. I also saw the waiter. I pointed him out to Matilda.

"Oh yes, what's his name again? Trip Rothery. You know, just because it seemed too obvious that he had the vial in his pocket doesn't mean he's not the perpetrator," Matilda said. "Agatha Christie used that device."

I was thoroughly confused. "What device do you mean?" I asked her.

"You know, the device where the murderer at first appeared to be framed. Agatha Christie used that device in *Hickory Dickory Dock*. However, most people think Agatha Christie always had the least likely suspect as the murderer, such as in *Lord Edgware Dies* or *Three Little Pigs*, but no, that was not always the case."

"I think the rain is easing a bit now," I said in an attempt to change the subject. All Matilda's talk of Agatha Christie and Miss Marple made my head spin. I usually couldn't follow her train of thought.

"So do you think it's the waiter?" Eleanor asked her.

"I certainly wouldn't dismiss him as a suspect," Matilda said. "Look, here he comes now. You'll have to speak to him, Jane, because you were present at the fatal dinner."

She pushed me forward into the rain, and I staggered into the waiter.

"I'm terribly sorry," I said.

"Don't I know you?" he said.

"Yes, I was at the dinner the other night when Marcus Matheson was murdered," I said.

"Oh yes." He seemed lost for words.

"Have the police arrested anyone yet?" I asked. He shook his head. "Do they have any suspects?"

"They suspected me for a time."

I feigned surprise. "Goodness me! Why would they do that?"

"Because the murderer slipped a vial of the poison into my jacket pocket somehow."

"That's terrible!" I said.

He readily agreed. "But the good thing was, my fingerprints weren't on it. And I wasn't wearing gloves, so the police knew it wasn't me. It had to be someone wearing gloves."

I was grateful that he was talking about that night, so I added, "The murderer had to be someone sitting at that table. I didn't notice anyone wearing gloves."

"Nor did I," he said, "and I thought about it a lot. Obviously they must've had a tissue or a handkerchief around the vial when they put it in my pocket. What's more, the murderer couldn't have drawn the poison from that particular vial."

"Why not?" I asked him.

"Because they would have had to use gloves and we didn't see anyone wearing gloves." The rain had changed direction and he adjusted his umbrella. "What I mean is, someone dropped the vial in my pocket to throw the suspicion onto me. They had already used a different vial to murder that poor man, and they would have hidden the evidence afterwards."

It took me a moment or two to follow his train of thought. "I see! It wasn't very clever of them to try to implicate you since no fingerprints where on the vial."

He nodded. "That's what the police said, luckily for me."

"I wonder who would want to kill him?" I asked, trying to not sound too keen to hear the answer.

"He wasn't well liked."

Now I was genuinely surprised. "He wasn't? Why wasn't he well liked?

"He might have been well liked in his personal life, but he certainly wasn't well liked in the restaurant business. His business was doing badly and that's why he had all those arguments with the chef."

"He argued publicly with Brendan Bowles?"

Trip nodded. "Brendan is quite a nasty man. He's always screaming at the staff, even when they haven't done anything wrong. If he comes to work in a bad mood, he takes it out on everyone."

"I heard that Marcus wouldn't allow Brendan to hire a full staff or buy top quality food in cost-cutting measures."

"That's right. The two of them were always at odds. I mean, Brendan is a nasty piece of work, but Marcus was cheap. Still, I can't suppose I could blame him for that when his business was going so badly."

"What about Candace and Rick Weatherspoon?"

He looked puzzled. "What do you mean?"

"Were their other businesses doing badly too?"

He shook his head. "No, they were trying to buy the business from Marcus, but he wanted to trade out of his bad financial situation. They were keen to buy his restaurants."

With that, he nodded and hurried away.

"Well done, Jane," Matilda said as she sloshed

through puddles to me. "That was excellent intelligence work."

"We need to find out about this Brendan Bowles," I said. "Still, the police would have all this information. I wish we could just leave it to them to solve."

"I know, but you did promise Cherri."

I groaned aloud. "Don't remind me."

"There's that handsome Scottish detective now," Matilda said with a wink. "Why don't you go and tell him what you've found out about Brendan Bowles and Marcus's finances."

"He probably already knows," I told her. "After all, he *is* a detective and we're just amateur sleuths."

"Speak for yourself," Matilda said. "I would count myself a little better than an amateur sleuth." With that, she winked at me again.

I thought it was a good idea to tell Detective McCloud what I had found out, but when I looked around, he had vanished. People were standing around talking, angling their umbrellas against the direction of the rain. A large pavilion tent had been erected near the gravesite. I could see Melissa standing under it being comforted by a group of women. I couldn't tell who they were from this distance, but I thought one of them was Candace Weatherspoon.

I thought things through again. Candace did have Botox parties and her husband was friends with the plastic surgeon, Dr. Davidson. What's more, while the nurse was administering the Botox, anyone would have had the opportunity to procure a few vials of Botox. Melissa and Candace were present at the Botox party, whereas the chef and the waiter weren't. Still, as the police had dismissed the waiter as a suspect, that only left Brendan. I needed to find out if he had a wife or if he had any connection whatsoever to Botox.

I was about to remark on this to Matilda when she snatched away my umbrella. "Eleanor and I are going to edge closer to the tent to see if we can overhear anything," she said. "It's best if I'm not seen talking to you for too long as I'm supposed to be a private detective, not your roommate. Thanks for the umbrella."

She was already a few steps away from me and clutching the umbrella tightly with both hands. I laughed and said, "You're welcome. I'll go and stand under a tree, I guess. Or maybe I'll just stay in the rain and die from hypothermia."

"Excellent. Oh, and Jane—keep your wits about

you and your eyes open." Matilda and Eleanor hurried over to the pavilion tent, taking my umbrella and all chance of dryness with them. The people not huddled under umbrellas congregated in the pavilion tent, and for a moment I thought about disobeying Matilda and joining them, if only to get warm. But I knew that was silly.

Instead, I scanned the cemetery, looking for the chef. I couldn't see him, but surely he would attend his boss's funeral. Most of the men looked alike given that they were all dressed in black suits and their hair was wet and plastered to their heads.

I walked over to a spreading hickory tree which afforded some shelter from the rain. The rain was unusually cold and I couldn't stop shivering in my little black dress, the only respectable clothing choice I had for such a solemn occasion. I was lost with my thoughts and jumped when I heard someone speak my name.

"Jane?" the voice said again, softer this time.

I turned around. "Oh, Detective McCloud." I tried not to sound too pleased to see him. "You scared the wits out of me."

"Damon." His voice was warm now as well as soft.

I smiled. "Damon."

"Err, did you forget your umbrella?" he asked me.

"Oh, no, I'm here with Matilda and Eleanor. They've got it." I waved my hand in the direction of the pavilion tent. "They stole it, actually. So if you're looking to make a bust…"

"I'll arrest them at once," he said with a smile. Then he went to give me his umbrella. "Take mine before you drown."

I waved both hands at him in protest. "I couldn't possibly. Thanks for the offer though. I'll just stick to sheltering from the rain under this tree."

"That's ridiculous." His voice was neither warm nor soft now. "You're freezing and you are drenched." Before I knew what was happening, he had taken off his coat and placed it around my shoulders.

The coat smelled like Damon, all woodlands and saffron.

I didn't know what to do, so I simply stammered, "Thank you, thank you." I stood there awkwardly, trying to not look too pleased with myself. A dashing detective giving me his coat. If only Ted could see me now.

Damon nodded over to the pavilion tent. "I see your ex-husband and his wife have just arrived."

Speak of the devil. I looked up to see Ted and Cherri. I had almost forgotten they would be at the funeral. As I watched, Cherri headed straight for Matilda and Eleanor. I figured she was asking where I was, because they pointed in my direction.

Cherri then made her way to me, stepping gingerly around the puddles in her impossibly high heels and clutching a flimsy white umbrella which was in imminent danger of collapsing under the rain. At least she had an umbrella, I thought bitterly.

"Yoo-hoo!" Cherri called out to me. "Darling Jane!"

"You seem to have made quite good friends with your ex-husband's wife," Damon said dryly.

"She was quite upset when Ted was taken in for questioning," I said. "She had no one to turn to and maybe she didn't trust Melissa Matheson or Candace Weatherspoon."

"Maybe not."

"I was just speaking with the waiter, Trip Rothery, a few minutes ago and he told me that Brendan Bowles had terrible arguments with Marcus

Matheson all the time. He was understaffed and Marcus wouldn't allow a sufficient budget for good quality food. But I suppose you knew that anyway."

Damon gave a half nod. "I hope you're not investigating in the hopes of protecting your ex-husband, Jane."

"I wouldn't care if my ex-husband went to jail forever," I said. And that was true, only I had promised Cherri, I would help. I wasn't about to tell the detective that, of course.

Cherri had reached us by now. She gasped when she saw Damon. "Oh Detective!" she said. "I didn't know it was you." She glanced down and blushed.

"Hello, Mrs. Delight," he said. "Goodbye for now, Jane." With that, Damon left me to my ex-husband's glowing young wife.

"Was he questioning you about the murder?" Cherri said.

I shook my head. "Do you have any more information for me?"

"No, I was hoping you'd have some information for me."

"Do you know the chef, Brendan Bowles?"

Cherri's umbrella twisted itself inside out and

she frantically tried to fix it. "I don't know him at all."

"So I don't suppose you know if he's married?"

"I wouldn't have a clue," Cherri said.

"These Botox parties that Candace has—did a woman by the surname of Bowles ever attend? Or did any of the women who attended ever say she had a husband who was a chef?"

Cherri appeared to be thinking it over. "Not to my knowledge. I don't know anyone by the name of Bowles and I don't know anyone whose husband is a chef."

I nodded, but Cherri asked me, "Do you think Brendan Bowles is the murderer?"

"No, but we have to consider everyone as a suspect," I told her.

Cherri had given up trying to fix her umbrella, and threw it to the ground in a huff. "What happened when Matilda questioned Melissa?"

"Melissa said she had taken out a life insurance policy on her husband ten years ago." I thought I should find out if Cherri had a life insurance policy on Ted just in case she was the murderer, so I added, "Of course, that isn't suspicious at all because wives always take out life insurance policies on their husbands. Does Ted have one?"

Cherri tapped her lip. "I don't know. He's never mentioned it."

"Are you sure?" I peered into her face.

"Yes, I think I'd remember if he'd said."

Just then I could hear classical music. Cherri grabbed my arm. "It looks like the funeral's starting. And Jane, why are you wearing that jacket? It's not very becoming, if you don't mind me saying so."

"Someone lent it to me because I was cold," I said.

She pulled my arm toward her. "You can share my umbrella."

The two of us walked over to the grave site under the remains of Cherri's umbrella. Melissa was standing in front next to the minister. She was clutching her black coat with one hand holding onto her black umbrella with the other. Brendan Bowles, the chef, was standing next to her and next to him was Candace Weatherspoon. I looked around, but could not see any sign of a woman next to Brendan.

Brendan himself did not appear to have used Botox or dermal fillers. His face looked perfectly untouched. It seemed unlikely to me that he was the murderer given that both Melissa and Candace had free access to Botox. Then again, maybe he had murdered Marcus with Botox for the very fact he knew Melissa and Candace had access to it.

The more I thought about it, the more it made sense. After all, someone had dropped a vial of Botox in Trip Rothery's pocket and that is how the police found out so soon that the poison was Botox.

Cherri pulled me over to Ted, who grunted at me. I assume he was saying *Hello.*

I grunted back. "Has your lawyer had a chance to look at those papers yet, Jane?" he whispered at me.

"Hardly appropriate talk for a funeral, Ted," I whispered back. "But if the police throw you in jail for Marcus's murder, I'm sure my lawyer won't mind sending the amendments to you there."

Ted looked shocked. I was glad Cherri hadn't heard me.

I edged away from them, still clutching Detective McCloud's coat to me. It smelled heavenly, like him, of the woods and of saffron. I wished I didn't have to give it back, and then I silently admonished myself for acting like a schoolgirl.

It was hard to hear what the minister was saying, despite the fact he had a microphone because the rain was absolutely crashing down. I edged closer and nearly bumped into Detective Stirling. I managed to circumnavigate him before he spoke to me. Thankfully for me, he seemed more interested in the service.

I positioned myself so I was standing directly behind Brendan Bowles so I could speak with him when he left. I looked over and could see Matilda and Eleanor standing nearly behind Weatherspoon. Matilda obviously knew what I was doing, and gave me a nod and a thumbs up.

As soon as the service was over people congregated around Melissa, leaving me clear to speak with the chef.

"Hello Mr. Bowles," I said as he made to walk past me. He looked at me. There was no sign of recognition in his face.

"I was at the table when Mr. Matheson passed away," I supplied. "I'm Ted Delight's ex-wife, Jane."

He held out his hand and I shook it. His grip was overly firm. I was glad I wasn't wearing rings because they would be crushed into my fingers. The feel of jewelry on my skin irritated me for some reason. I figured it was due to the fact I'd been raised Amish and Amish don't wear jewelry, not even buttons. I had spent the first sixteen years of my life without it. Of course, the Amish reason was vanity.

"A sad matter," he said.

"Yes it is," I agree. "I hope the police catch the murderer soon."

"So do I," he said. "And Marcus wouldn't be happy that Melissa intends to sell the business to Candace and Rick."

"She is?" I said. "Yes, Marcus certainly would not be happy about that. I know he had business problems, but he wanted to trade out of them."

Red splotches appeared on Brendan's face. "Yes, Marcus would turn in his grave. It was because of the debt, mind you, but it was impossible to run the restaurant with the budget he enforced on us. Candace and Rick will do a much better job. Hopefully, they'll be able to trade out of the mess the business is in."

"So you think they'll be able to save it?"

Brendan nodded vigorously. "They have plenty of money, whereas Marcus was practically skint."

"Really?" I said. "I knew the business was bad, but I didn't know he was going broke."

"It's no secret," Brandon said. "I'm sure it wouldn't have been long before they foreclosed on his house."

I pointed to a random lady standing nearby. "Is that your wife over there?"

Brendan chuckled. "No, my wife and I divorced a year ago and it was a nasty divorce. It's put me off women for a while, I can tell you, no offense."

I forced a chuckle. So Brendan didn't have a female friend who could obtain the Botox from one of Candace's parties. Still, Brendan seemed to be on good terms with Candace and Rick.

A man approached, clearly wanting to speak with Brendan, so I smiled and walked away. If only I had found out more from Brendan. He had confirmed what we had heard about Marcus's business going downhill, but I was surprised to learn the news of Marcus's financial affairs.

After Brendan and the man shook hands, I saw him walk over to speak with Dr. Davidson. They shook hands warmly and Dr. Davidson patted Brendan on his shoulder. Brendan said something and the doctor laughed. They certainly didn't look like people who were upset over someone's funeral.

There was my direct link. There was no need for Brendan to have a wife or girlfriend who could obtain the Botox from one of Candace's parties—he could go straight to the source, Dr. Davidson.

CHAPTER 16

That evening, Matilda, Eleanor, and I were sitting in our apartment. Eleanor had put the cat activity tree next to the pole so Mr. Crumbles could slide down, and he was having a lot of fun doing so.

"You'll have to move that before Cherri comes," Matilda scolded her. "It's just not at all safe, the way he flies off at the end."

"But he enjoys it," Eleanor protested.

Matilda rolled her eyes. "That's beside the point as you well know. It's simply not safe for anyone. Now where could Cherri be? She's five minutes late."

I smiled to myself. Matilda did not like people being late. That, and the fact that she did everything with military precision, made me wonder if she had been in the military in her youth.

Mr. Crumbles flew through the air once more, his legs outstretched, looking for all the world like a giant bat. "I think he's covering more distance with practice," Matilda said in alarm.

I stood up when the bell to the apartment rang. "I'll get it," I said. "It must be Cherri. Eleanor, are you moving that activity tree now?"

"Yes, Mr. Crumbles has had enough fun for the night." Eleanor scooped him up and took him away, presumably to give him some treats.

I breathed a sigh of relief. Without the activity tree, Mr. Crumbles could not reach the top of the pole.

When I reached the front door, I opened it a tiny crack and said, "Cherri, come in quickly, won't you. Mr. Crumbles always tries to make a run for it."

"Yes, I'm always careful, Jane, darling." She came inside and air kissed me on both cheeks. "I've brought chocolates and wine," she announced proudly.

"That's very kind of you. Please come in." I locked the door behind her and we made our way up the stairs.

As we walked up the stairs, I wondered when Detective McCloud—I still found it hard to think of him as Damon—would come to collect his coat. I had taken it to the dry cleaners that afternoon. Truth be told, I wished I could have stayed in it all afternoon with it wrapped around me. I probably would have, if it hadn't been so wet.

"Matilda and Eleanor darling," Cherri said by way of greeting. "It's wonderful to see you. Ted was ever so suspicious about you being a private detective."

"Was he suspicious of my fake name, Miss Marple?" Matilda asked her.

A look of confusion passed across Cherri's face. "No. Why would he be suspicious?"

Matilda shook her head. "Never mind. Did he believe you?"

"Of course he does. Ted always believes me. He never thinks I'm lying."

I raised my eyes. I wondered if in fact Cherri had ever lied to Ted. Her tone was entirely too smug.

"Yes, he asked me again and again where your offices were and I said I couldn't remember. And then he asked me how I found you and I said on the internet. You have no idea what it's like to be married to a lawyer. They give you the third degree at every opportunity."

"Yes, I'm only too well aware," I said. The irony appeared to be lost on Cherri. After all, I had been married to the man for decades, a fact which seemed to be eluding her at the present moment.

"Well isn't this fun, our own little murder club just like Aurora Teagarden," Cherri said.

Matilda's face lit up. "I do love Aurora Teagarden."

"Cherri brought chocolates and wine," I announced. I headed to the kitchen.

"Where are you going, Jane darling?" Cherri asked me.

"To make coffee and fetch the chocolate beet cake," I said.

"But darling, I brought wine," she said. "Bring some wine glasses, won't you?"

I switched on the coffee machine. Mr. Crumbles was sitting there giving me his usual look. I wondered what it meant. I just knew he was up to something. I wanted to stay on his good side, so I gave him some treats.

Unfortunately, Eleanor spied me. "What are you doing?" she called out.

"Giving Mr. Crumbles some treats," I said.

"You should use them sparingly because we don't want him to get too fat," Eleanor lectured me.

Sorry," I said. Still, if I had to be on someone's good side, I'd rather be on Mr. Crumbles than Eleanor's.

I took wine glasses and the chocolate beet cake to the living room. "Lovely funeral service today wasn't it," Cherri said.

We all mumbled agreement.

Matilda cleared her throat. "Now, this is what we found out so far."

I waved to Matilda to interrupt her. "Cherri, there's something we have to tell you about Ted."

She went white. "He's not having an affair, is he?"

I hesitated, because how on earth would I know whether or not he was. It certainly wouldn't be the first time.

"No, of course not," Matilda said in a firm voice, but then added, "Not that we know. It's just I found out some information from Ted and I suggested he tell you first. Has he told you about his brother?"

"He did say he had something to tell me about his brother, but he hasn't told me what it is yet."

Matilda and I exchanged glances. "We have to tell her," I said.

Cherri's hand flew to her throat. "What is it? How bad is it?"

"It's just that many years ago Ted was arrested for being in possession of recreational drugs. He didn't want to become a lawyer with that on his record, so he gave the police his brother's name."

Cherri did not look surprised, but maybe she'd simply had too much Botox at the party the other night.

"And Ted paid his brother a lot of money, so they both got what they wanted, I suppose," I added.

Cherri appeared to be processing the information. Her face flushed pink and then she took a large gulp of wine. I pushed the box of chocolates over to her and she ate one before speaking. "Ted didn't tell me." She looked to be on the verge of tears.

"He was probably horribly embarrassed," I said. "He was afraid you'd think badly of him."

"Why are you defending your ex-husband?" Eleanor asked me.

"I'm not defending him at all; I just don't want Cherri to be upset," I told Eleanor.

Cherri tapped both her ears. "I can hear you. I'm right here. I don't understand why Ted didn't tell me, especially when he thinks I hired you, Matilda."

"I did ask him to tell you," Matilda said.

Cherri's face softened. "Poor Popsicle. He must be so terribly afraid to tell me. I just want to run home right now and give him a big hug."

I pulled a face and shook my head. This was all too much.

"Why don't we talk about the suspects," I said, hoping to change the subject to something more cheerful than Ted's indiscretions and crimes.

"Yes. Who do you think it is?" Cherri said.

"My guess is Brendan Bowles. He had the motive and the opportunity, and he has a direct link to Botox as he appears to know Dr. Davidson quite well. I saw the two of them acting quite friendly with each other at the funeral. They're certainly not strangers, at any rate."

Cherri poured herself another glass of wine. "So the people who had access to the Botox were Brendan, Melissa, and Candace."

"And Rick," I reminded her. "He's also friends with Dr. Davidson."

"Maybe they were all in it together," Matilda

said gleefully. "Maybe Dr. Davidson, Rick, Candace, and Melissa all did it. The same sort of thing happened on *Murder on the Orient Express*, if you recall. Everyone always thinks there is only one murderer, and that confuses people. When you open your mind to the possibility that there could be more than one murderer, then it becomes obvious, doesn't it?"

I frowned. "Not really. I must say, I'm a little confused. You really don't think all four of them murdered Marcus, do you?" I asked Matilda.

She shrugged. "I have no idea, but perhaps each of them had a reason to do away with the vic."

I turned to Cherri. "Cherri, were you aware that Marcus's finances were in a terrible state?"

She shot me an absent look. "I think Ted did mention that to me."

"Then Melissa would have a lot to gain if she murdered him. Marcus was in danger of losing the house and losing his businesses. He stubbornly wanted to trade out of his financial position, but the chef said he wouldn't have been able to. He refused to sell the businesses to Candace and Rick, but now that Marcus has gone, Melissa hasn't wasted any time agreeing to sell his businesses."

"That's not suspicious in itself," Matilda said, "because what else would a level-headed person do under such circumstances?"

I selected a strawberry cream chocolate and swallowed it before answering. "You're right. Besides, she took out that life insurance policy on her husband ten years ago. No one would plot a murder ten years prior to committing it."

"Then we're back to Rick, Candace, and the chef," Eleanor said.

"But what about the waiter?" Cherri asked me.

"He's already been discounted by the police," I said. "I find it strange that someone would try to frame him. It would soon be discovered that he couldn't have done it, so what was the point in trying to frame him? It doesn't make sense."

Matilda tapped her chin. "Maybe the murderer wasn't trying to frame him," she said. "Maybe the murderer wanted the police to know the poison was Botox."

I shook my head. "Now you've really lost me. What possible motive would the murderer have for doing that?"

"I'm not sure yet," Matilda said. "It often takes Miss Marple some time to put the pieces together, but she always does in the end. There's something not right about it. You know, it seems to me the murderer did want the police to know the poison was Botox."

"Let's brainstorm the advantages of doing that. The one that springs to mind is that it would advance the case."

Cherri looked at me. "What do you mean?"

"I mean the police would know at once he was murdered with Botox. They would waste no time looking for natural causes. But how could that benefit the murderer?"

We all fell silent for a few moments, but no one came up with a solution.

"What's the next move?" Cherri said.

"I don't know," Matilda admitted. "I agree with Jane that the chef is the likeliest suspect. Chefs take pride in their work. The restaurant was understaffed, and Marcus wouldn't give him the budget for quality food. That would have put his career in jeopardy."

"But would someone murder someone over such a thing?" Cherri asked.

Matilda shrugged. "That's the million-dollar question, isn't it?"

"What do we do next?" Cherri asked us again.

"I'd like to speak with Candace and ask her

some hard questions," I said. "Unless Matilda wants to go in disguise again as a private detective."

"We can't do it tomorrow because we have the fundraiser," Matilda said.

I gasped. "Fundraising? You didn't mention it to me!" I certainly hoped she wouldn't mention calendars.

"Yes, we did," Matilda protested. "You know, the goats."

"Coats?"

Matilda shook her head. "No, goats at the petting zoo in the park. Didn't you hear me mention it to Rebecca?"

"I did hear you saying something about it, but didn't realize it was so soon."

Matilda turned to Cherri. "Tomorrow Eleanor and I are helping with the fundraiser. There's going to be a petting zoo with goats."

I trembled. I was certain something would go wrong.

Matilda, Eleanor, and goats. I shook my head. That was a recipe for disaster.

CHAPTER 17

$\mathcal{W}$hen I awoke the next morning, my neck was sore again. I figured I had once more slept badly from stress, but this time it wasn't from stress over the murder; it was from stress over Matilda, Eleanor, and the goats.

As a child, my family had two milking goats and I knew just how mischievous and naughty goats could be. They were filled with personality. Given the fact that Matilda and Eleanor had the same type of cheeky personality, I couldn't shake the feeling that something untoward was going to happen.

As I staggered out of the bathroom, Matilda thrust a coffee cup into my hands.

"Denki," I said, for some reason lapsing into

Pennsylvania Dutch. I followed it by the translation, "Thank you."

I took a sip of the coffee and smiled. Matilda really did make wonderful coffee.

"Now hurry, everyone. We don't have much time to waste. We have to get there to set up."

"Just what type of animals will be at the petting zoo?" I asked suspiciously.

Eleanor shot me a blank look. "We don't know. There will be chickens of course, and I think a miniature pony for children to pat."

"Well, what else would children do with a miniature pony if not pat her?" Matilda said with a rude snort. "It *is* called a petting zoo, after all."

"It's not called a patting zoo. Besides, children ride ponies."

"They don't ride miniature ponies because they're too small. That's why they're called *miniature*." Matilda's tone was derisive.

"It depends on the size of the pony and the size of the child," Eleanor pointed out. "Honestly, Matilda I hope your mood improves."

So do I, I said silently. Aloud I said, "So where did you get these goats. Did Rebecca recommend somewhere?"

They both looked at each other and then at me. Eleanor said in a puzzled tone, "Rebecca?"

"Maybe we should have asked her," Matilda said. "I had no idea she would know where we could borrow some goats."

"Many Amish people have their own milking cow or a couple of milking goats," I told her.

When they didn't respond, I pressed them for an answer. "So where did you happen to find goats? Are they dairy goats or are they fiber goats?

Eleanor frowned. "I don't know what a fiber goat is." Even Mr. Crumbles who was sitting next to her on the couch stared at me in his unblinking way, as if puzzled by my words.

"An angora goat or a cashmere goat," I told them. "You know that goats are used for mohair and cashmere. And then there are dairy goats and then meat goats."

Eleanor put both hands over Mr. Crumbles' ears.

"They're rescue goats," Matilda said.

"Rescue goats?" I repeated. "Where did you get them?"

Matilda drew her hand across her brow. "We rescued them."

The sinking feeling settled in the pit of my

stomach. "Where exactly did you rescue them from?"

"They were going off to be, well you know, eaten." Matilda glanced at Eleanor who put her hands over Mr. Crumbles' ears once more. "We couldn't have that, so we bought fifteen of them."

"You bought them!" I shrieked. "Where on earth are you going to keep them?"

"That's where Rebecca did come in handy," Eleanor said. "You said you overheard us mentioning the petting zoo fundraiser to her the other day."

"Yes, but I wasn't paying attention," I said. "What exactly is Rebecca going to do with these goats?"

"We've hired a field for the goats until we find good homes for them."

"But Matilda, that might be a very long time," I said reasonably and slowly, as if talking to a recalcitrant child. "Most people have cats or dogs as pets, not goats. Besides, do you have any idea how naughty goats are? They love to jump up and down on cars. They love to eat potted plants and anything in the garden that they shouldn't eat."

"I'll train them," Eleanor protested.

A horrible thought struck me. "These are wild goats, aren't they?"

"That's a bit judgmental, dear," Matilda said. "They've just had a difficult upbringing."

I sat on the nearest chair and put my head between my hands. I had figured there was something wrong with this. Matilda and Eleanor had bought fifteen wild goats. Not only were they going to put them in a petting zoo, they were going to take them to Rebecca's farm afterwards.

"You do realize goats can jump fences?" I asked them. "They might not stay in Rebecca's field for long. Goats can jump high and they're very good at climbing. Besides, they're browsers, not grazers so they like to eat leaves and branches more so than grass. And then their hooves need doing, and they need deworming and vaccinating."

"A vet can do that," Matilda said.

"And how do you propose to catch the wild goats?" I asked her.

"Goodness gracious me, enough of the judgment, Jane!" Matilda exclaimed. "These are perfectly nice goats. They will realize they have come to a good home and will be on their best behaviour."

I wished I could be somewhere else, maybe

fleeing from a murderer, anything to be away from this whole goat situation.

When we arrived at the park, the scene that greeted us was peaceful, much to my relief. A big sign at the front announced this was a fundraiser for the local fire station. I hadn't even asked what the fundraiser was for but now it made sense. Matilda and Eleanor were clearly helping their friend, Gene, but surely they could have found another way to do it.

We walked past a cheery man with crates of chickens and a happy family with a crate of turkeys. Clearly these were pets. We continued on under some trees, past a crate with a peaceful, sleeping pig. That was when I heard goats bleating.

"I wonder why he delivered them to the building?" Eleanor asked Matilda. "It's such a lovely day and everyone had decided to have the petting zoo outside unless it rained."

I walked inside the long brick building and gasped.

A high mesh wire fence was in front of me, and behind it were fifteen clearly wild goats of every size and shape. Their hair stuck out in all directions, and they had long, scraggly beards. They certainly were a motley assortment.

One of them looked at me with big yellow eyes and bleated.

I looked back at Matilda to see she was speaking to a man. "Thanks for delivering them," she said as she counted out a bunch of bills to him. "So you'll be back in five hours to collect them and deliver them to the farm?"

"Sure," he said, handing her a key. "This is for the padlock. Be careful with them, won't you? I told you they're wild. We don't handle them at all. We just breed them and sell them to the meat market."

Eleanor gasped. "The poor little things."

The goats were running around crazily. One was jumping up and down on the spot. I looked again and realized the goat was trying to jump out the window high above.

"I've given them water, as you can see." He pointed to a water trough. "And those are the bags of grain over there."

Matilda opened her purse again, but he said, "No, you already paid me for that." He handed her a receipt, and then hurried out the door.

"How are you going to feed them without going in there?" I asked them. "I don't think you should open the gate. These goats will be better than Mr. Crumbles at escaping."

Matilda and Eleanor both looked discomfited. "I know, we'll throw the hay over the fence to them," Matilda said.

I looked at the fence. It wasn't too tall, but it was certainly tall enough to prevent the goats jumping out—at least I hoped so. Call me optimistic. "That's a good idea," I said, at the same time wondering if it was.

I walked over to a bale of hay. The man had already opened it. Matilda, Eleanor, and I threw the bale of hay to the goats bit by bit. The goats munched it hungrily.

"Great, that's calmed them down," Eleanor said.

"How can anyone pat those goats?" I asked them.

"Why like this, of course," Eleanor said. She walked up to the goats and pushed her hand through the wire. To my surprise, she was able to pat a nearby goat that was greedily munching hay. "As long as we keep them fed, I think someone can pat them."

I shook my head. "It's going to be awfully hard to capture those goats if they escape."

I wasn't looking forward to a day of guarding goats that were likely to escape at the first opportunity. I had visions of them running around town, creating havoc.

I shook my head. I shouldn't imagine the worst happening. Maybe they wouldn't escape. Maybe this would all go smoothly. The man would return and transport them to Rebecca's farm where they would stay in a field and not jump out and live happily ever after.

Yes, I was sure that would happen. I smiled and nodded, trying to convince myself.

"Jane, would you mind the goats while Eleanor and I get some coffee? We'll bring you back a coffee too of course. Maybe something to eat?"

"That would be great, thanks. I'm ravenous," I said. "Just bring me anything."

After they left, I walked over to check the padlock, just as a young woman hurried inside the building after five enthusiastic children. "They're not all mine," she said to me.

I smiled. "The goats aren't terribly friendly, I'm afraid. Maybe if the children take a piece of hay and poke it through the wire, the goats will come up to them, but make sure they don't put their fingers through the wire."

The children all took a piece of hay and pushed

it through the wire. It wasn't long before the goats were taking hay from the children.

I was enormously relieved. Maybe this might work out after all.

I watched as the goats became braver, sticking their faces against the wire to get every last piece of hay.

A shriek startled me. "What have they done?" the woman yelled.

I looked up to see the youngest child. He must have had his head pushed against the wire because the goats had eaten his hair.

His hair looked terrible, his original long strands of hair sitting next to pieces of almost bald scalp. He looked like the lead singer in an extreme heavy metal band. The child did not appear to care, but the woman was almost crying. "My sister will kill me!" she wailed. She shot me an accusing look.

I simply sat there dumbstruck. "A goat ate your hair," one child told the victim.

The victim's face lit up. "Really?" he said, touching his hair and smiling widely. The woman grabbed the child's hand and took him out the door, followed by the other children who were all doubled over with laughter.

I knew something bad would happen. To make

it worse, Matilda and Eleanor were certainly taking their time with my breakfast and coffee. I figured they had been side tracked and had abandoned me to babysit the goats.

I heard footsteps and brightened, but to my surprise it was Detective McCloud.

"Detective McCloud," I said, by way of greeting.

"Damon, please," he said.

"Damon." My heart was beating out of my chest so loudly that I was afraid he would be able to hear it. I always did feel rather off-balance in the detective's presence.

"Are you guarding goats?" he asked with a laugh.

At least, that's what I thought he said in his thick Scottish accent. Maybe he was asking about his coat. "Your coat's at the dry cleaners," I told him. "It will be back tomorrow."

"You didn't have to do that," he said.

"It was kind of you to lend it to me. Are you here to question me more about the murder?"

"No," he began, but Matilda burst in the door. "Sorry I took so long," she said.

When she saw Detective McCloud, she stood stock-still. "Am I interrupting something?"

"Oh no, no," I stammered.

She hurried over and handed me a polystyrene cup of coffee and a cream cheese bagel. "Have the goats been good?"

"Not at all." I explained what happened to the child's hair.

"Oh yes, I saw that woman out there complaining. I wondered what all the fuss was about. She's making a mountain out of a molehill. It could easily be fixed by shaving that child's head. I'll go out and offer to shave his head now."

I put a restraining hand on her arm. "Maybe it's just best if you let her go on her way," I said.

"These goats don't look very friendly," Damon said. He put his hand through the wire mesh and wiggled his fingers through the wire mesh. The goats all stood at the back of the building and stared at him warily.

"If you push hay through the mesh, they'll come up to you," I said. I walked over to the little haystack and pulled some out of another bale. I stuck it through the mesh and the goats hurried over, jostling one another to reach the hay first.

CHAPTER 18

I was lying stretched out on the couch with my feet elevated and a cold pack on my forehead. Still, every time I shut my eyes I could see wild goats running around.

I heard someone speaking so I took the cold pack off my eyes.

It was Matilda. "We're going to our card game now," she said. "We'll be away for a few hours."

"I didn't know you played bridge," I said.

She glared at me. "I don't. It's poker."

"I should have known." I put the cold pack back on my forehead. Moments later, I heard a swishing sound. I peeped out behind the cold pack just in time to see Mr. Crumbles airborne, all four paws outstretched. "Eleanor, would you please move the cat activity tree away from the pole before you leave?"

"No time, sorry Jane. We're terribly late. Would you mind doing it?" With that, Eleanor disappeared down the stairs, as did Matilda.

I struggled off the couch and made my way into the kitchen to fetch Mr. Crumbles a treat. He was already sitting there with an expectant look on his face. I gave him some treats and was halfway across the living room to remove the cat activity tree when I heard a phone ring.

It was not my ring tone. In fact, it sounded like Matilda's. I frantically searched for it and found it under a skateboard magazine on the coffee table. I really had to wonder about Matilda and Eleanor's reading matter.

I didn't recognize the Caller ID, but thought I had better answer it. I knew Matilda wouldn't mind.

"This is Candace Weatherspoon," the voice began. "That's not you, Matilda, is it?"

"Candace, it's Jane," I said. "Matilda's just gone out. She left her phone here." I wondered why Candace would call Matilda. "Can I take a message?"

Candace sounded breathless. "Cherri told me

Matilda is a private investigator," she said. "She gave me her number. Cherri said Matilda is doing some private investigating for her."

"That's right," I said. *Sort of,* I added silently.

Candace pushed on in the same breathless voice. "I think I know who the murderer is."

"Have you gone to the police?"

"No, because I could be completely wrong. It's just that something occurred to me and I'm not sure if it has anything to do with the murder or not, but it made me think."

"What is it?" I asked her.

"Her best friend in junior high stole her boyfriend, and she waited ten years to get back at her. She planned it for a whole ten years."

"I'm afraid I don't understand," I said, thinking I should perhaps have some Advil.

"Jane, you say Matilda isn't there? I really wanted to speak with her. I was hoping she could come by now."

"You can talk to me," I said. "Matilda and I discuss the case all the time."

"Could you come over, Jane?" she asked.

"Sure," I said. Just then, there was a strange sound and the phone went dead.

I looked at the phone. Had she simply hung up?

It was the usual place to end a conversation after all. Or had she been attacked? What if the murderer was there at this very minute? Should I call the police?

I stood there, my hand over my mouth, looking at Matilda's phone for some time. It was probably nothing to worry about. I called her back, but the phone went straight to voicemail. Maybe she was on another call. I left a voicemail asking her to call me back and telling her I was on my way.

I decided to drive straight to Candace's house. I remembered the way from when I had been there at the Botox party the other night.

On my way, I thought things through. Candace had mentioned a woman taking revenge. Surely she was referring to Melissa. There was no other female suspect in the case, was there? Then it dawned on me—Cherri.

Could Cherri be the murderer? What if Cherri had planned to steal my then-husband and have a baby with him to trap him? He was wealthy, after all. What if she had taken out a life insurance policy on him and planned to murder him?

If that was the case, then why did she ask my help in solving the murder? I had no idea, but maybe she had reasons of her own. Maybe she wanted to befriend me so I would not be suspicious of her when she did away with Ted.

I thought about it all the way to Candace's house, but no answers came to mind, only more questions.

When I reached Candace's house, I knocked loudly and called out. No one answered. I called out about another five times. I tried the front door but it was locked. I skirted around to the back of the house and walked along by the pool, calling out as I went.

I tried the first door I saw at the back of the house. It opened into an expensive kitchen, showcasing wall after wall of stainless steel and granite countertops.

I called out again but couldn't see anyone. Now I really was getting worried. Something just didn't seem right. I walked into the room where the Botox party had been held. There was not a soul in sight. I ran up the staircase, sprinting down the hallway, and stuck my head into each of the six bedrooms. There was not a sign of anyone.

That was when I remembered the pool house. Of course, someone had said that Rick and Dr. Davidson were in the pool house. I hurried down the stairs, taking them two at a time outside. I had assumed the pool house was detached from the house, but now I realized it was actually adjoining. I ran to it and flung open the front door.

There to my horror, was Candace lying on the floor, blood oozing from her head. I snatched my phone out of my purse as I hurried to her, calling 911 one as I ran.

I touched her shoulder, and she groaned. Thank goodness, she was alive!

After I called them, I called Damon and told him what had happened.

"Jane, the perpetrator could still be in the house. Run to your car and lock yourself in."

"I can't leave her," I protested.

"But the paramedics are on the way. I'm in the neighborhood, just a few minutes away. Jane, please return to your car." His tone was pleading.

I can't," I said again. I hung up and turned my attention to Candace. I inspected the gash on the side of her head. It was deep and would need stitches but wasn't bleeding freely. I grabbed a towel and ran it under cold water and then pressed it onto her head.

She opened her eyes. "Ouch! Is that you, Jane?"

"Yes, lie quietly," I said. "The paramedics are on their way." I hurried over to a nearby couch to grab a cushion which I gently placed it under her head.

"What happened?" she asked me.

"You've had a nasty knock on the head," I told her. "You don't remember what happened?"

"No."

"Don't worry, that can happen with a blow to the head," I said, hazarding a guess. "I'm sure you'll be able to remember in a day or two. Now try not to move. That's going to hurt."

"It hurts now," she said. I repositioned the towel against the injury site.

"What are you doing here?" she asked me.

"You called me and asked me to come over," I told her. "You called for Matilda, but she was out so I said I'd come instead. You thought you knew who the murderer was."

"Yes I did, but I can't remember now. I just remember I was shocked when I realized it was her."

"A woman?" I asked, and she gave a little shrug.

I heard sirens approaching in the distance. "You said it was someone who waited a long time to take revenge," I told her, and would have said more, but I realized the sirens were directly outside the house.

I hurried to the door so I could show Damon

where we were. When I was halfway to the door, I heard someone go out the back door. I hesitated and then ran outside. Damon had just driven past. I waved my arms.

"There was someone in there with us," I told him as soon as he jumped out of the vehicle. "They ran out the back door just then." I pointed to the pool house. Damon sprinted past me and kept going. The paramedics arrived at that point, so I waved my arms at them as well.

They were working on Candace when Damon returned. "I couldn't catch them," he said.

"Did you see them at all?" I asked him.

"No, but Jane it's lucky I came along when I did. Who knows what would have happened to you?"

"I was in there with Candace for some time," I said, wondering why the murderer hadn't attacked me. That's when it occurred to me—maybe the murderer had somehow discovered that Candace wanted to give Matilda information and was waiting for me to arrive so she could find out how much I did in fact know. I shuddered.

One of the paramedics wheeled Candace out while the other remained to speak with Damon. "She's not too bad, just a nasty gash on the head that will need stitches. She also has a concussion, but nothing life-threatening. You should be able to question her in a few hours."

"But she can't remember anything," I told him. "Anything at all?"

"She did know who I was," I said, "but we had a conversation on the phone before I arrived. She can't remember what that was about."

"That's quite common in head trauma victims," he said. "Do you know how it happened?"

"Yes, I believe someone hit her over the head with that." I indicated a large wooden candlestick lying on the floor nearby. The top of it was covered with blood.

The paramedic and Damon spoke for a few more minutes and then Damon turned to me after the paramedic left. "I'll need a witness statement from you, Jane. I'll call by later."

"Damon, there's something you need to know. Cherri asked for my help in solving the murder."

Damon looked quite cross. He put his hands on his hips and drew himself to his full height.

"I didn't want to help Cherri at all. It's just that she seemed so upset and didn't know anyone else in town. We promised we would help her. Matilda pretended to be a private investigator."

"Yes, I figured as much."

"The thing is, Candace called me earlier wanting to speak to Matilda. She actually thought Matilda a private investigator and that Cherri had, in fact, hired her. I told her Matilda was out for the afternoon and she could tell me whatever she had to say."

"And what did she say?" Damon asked me.

"She didn't make any sense. She said she thought she knew who the murderer was. I suggested she tell the police, but she said it was only a hunch and she wanted to tell me about it to get my opinion. She said someone had taken revenge for something that happened to her in junior high ten years ago."

Damon quirked one eyebrow. "Is that all she said?"

I nodded. "Yes, I know it doesn't make any sense. And now she can't remember. She does remember saying that, but she can't remember who it was about. And something else is bothering me. The person who attacked Candace was still in the pool house while I was here. Do you think they were waiting to see how much she told me?"

"Possibly," Damon said. "This is a serious situation, Jane. I hope you realize that."

"Yes I do," I said solemnly. "What happens now?"

"Go back home and leave this to me. I'll check on you later when I take your witness statement. Are you able to drive yourself home?"

"I'm fine," I said. "I'm worried about Candace. What if the murderer tries to finish her off?"

"I'll have an officer stationed at the hospital," Damon said. "But for now Jane, go home and leave this to me."

I made to leave but turned back to him. "It seems the murderer is a woman," I told him.

"Yes," he said. "And that means it's either Cherri or Melissa."

$\mathcal{J}$ drove home quite shaken. I had left several messages on Eleanor's phone, but she hadn't called me back. Who could the murderer be? Matilda had told me that murderers in Agatha Christie books sometimes pretend to have a close escape so that suspicion will not fall on them, but that gash on Candace's head was deep. I was certain it couldn't have been self-inflicted. I hardly thought she would hit herself on the head so hard just to throw suspicion off herself. Besides, I had heard someone running from the scene.

But was it Cherri or Melissa? I had no idea.

I carefully let myself into the apartment, but there was no sign of Mr. Crumbles. I found him asleep, curled up in a chair. I tiptoed past him, put my purse on the coffee table, and lay on the couch with my feet up once more. The cold pack was now lukewarm, so I left it where it was sitting. This had certainly been an eventful day.

I decided to sort through the facts. What had Candace said? She said someone had waited ten years to take revenge. In fact, she said they had planned their revenge for ten years. I nodded slowly. Yes, that was important.

Was Cherri planning to murder Ted? And what would her motive be for killing Marcus? As far as I knew, she had never met him. Ted had never introduced me to any of his business associates. But then again, he might have introduced Cherri. And what possible grudge could she have had against Marcus?

The bell to the apartment rang, startling me. I groaned and got to my feet. All I wanted was a nice quiet afternoon. That obviously wasn't going to happen. I walked down the stairs wondering if it was Damon so soon.

I peeped around the door. To my surprise, it was Melissa Matheson.

"May I come in?" She asked me.

I hesitated. Should I slam the door in her face and lock it? There was a fifty percent chance she was the murderer. As I was thinking up an excuse not to let her in, she pushed past me and said, "Thank you."

I had no option but to follow her up the stairs and keep my wits about me.

"Would you like coffee or a drink?" I asked her.

She shook her head. "I think I might know who the murderer is, and Cherri told me she hired the services of your roommate, Matilda."

I wondered why Cherri told Melissa. "Please sit down," I said.

Instead of sitting in the empty chair, she pushed Mr. Crumbles off and sat down where he had been lying asleep.

Mr. Crumbles landed on the floor with a thud. He shook himself before turning around and shooting her a nasty look. She appeared not to notice.

I thought it quite mean of her to do that to Mr. Crumbles. After all, there was a seat right next to her.

"Jane," she said. "Did you hear what I just said?"

"No," I admitted.

"It's quite difficult. I really don't know how to tell you."

"Well just say it," I said. The woman was beginning to irritate me.

"I think it's Cherri."

"Cherri?" I repeated. "Why would you think it was Cherri?"

"Because I think Cherri is a con artist who married Ted so she could murder him some time in the distant future and get his money. He is a wealthy man, isn't he?"

"Yes," I said. "But couldn't she just divorce him? Why would she have to murder him?"

Melissa made a clicking sound with her tongue. "Obviously, Ted would have made her sign a pre-nup. She won't get a cent in a divorce. I assume you didn't either." She gestured around the apartment. I thought that quite rude of her. I simply nodded.

"So the only way for Cherri to get her hands on his money is to do away with him."

"But Cherri doesn't seem to want for anything now," I pointed out. "She seems to have anything she wants."

"Ted told me you were brought up Amish. I can see you're still not fully aware of the ways of the world," Melissa said in a condescending tone. "Ted is significantly older than Cherri. If she murders Ted, she can go on to the next wealthy, older victim.

Some women do this in a serial fashion, you understand."

"But surely they get caught."

Melissa shrugged one shoulder. "Murderers don't always get caught." There was something smug about her tone. "Haven't you seen all those cold cases on TV that are never solved?"

"Yes I have, but I don't understand why Cherri would kill Marcus. It doesn't make any sense. What possible motive could she have had?"

"Because Marcus was a lawyer before he became a restaurateur," she said. "You probably don't know this, but he defended Cherri's mother in a case and lost. The poor woman went bankrupt and so Cherri held a grudge against him. It was many years ago, when Cherri was just a child."

"What was the case about?" I asked her.

She waved her hand at me. "How should I know? I was lucky to find out that much. The police kept questioning me, and I think they suspect me, so I decided to do some digging into the case. I was able to find this out rather easily, but if the police don't arrest Cherri soon, I'm going to hire a private detective of my own. It's her, you mark my words. She'd been planning to kill Marcus for the last ten years and finally she got the opportunity."

"Ten years," I said. The timeframe stuck in my mind. Why did it sound so familiar to me? I tapped my chin. "Ten years," I repeated slowly, staring at the ceiling.

That's when it dawned on me. Melissa had taken out the life insurance policy on Marcus ten years earlier. My skin went cold. The murderer wasn't Cherri after all—the murderer was Melissa. And what's more, she was sitting in the apartment with me.

I wondered how I could get out of the apartment in a hurry. "Would you like some cupcakes?" I asked her. "I always think better on a full stomach. I'll just pop downstairs to the cupcake store and grab some."

I stood up and made to move past her, but she grabbed my arm. "You know, don't you!"

I plastered an innocent look across my face. "Know what?" I asked her.

"There's no use pretending, Jane. You have a very expressive face. I saw the moment you realized it was me."

I backed away from her.

"I was hoping I could convince you it was Cherri."

"But what happens when Candace remembers it was you who hit her over the head?"

"I didn't hit her hard enough, obviously," she said. "I'm on my way to pay her a little visit. Maybe I'll smother her with a pillow or inject something into her IV. Besides, even if I fail in my next attempt, no one's going to believe someone who's already lost their memory."

She pulled out a gun and trained it on me. I noticed it had a silencer.

The room spun, and I thought I would faint. Damon had said he would check on me later. I needed to keep her talking. I hoped Damon would hurry.

"So, have you really been planning to murder your husband for the last ten years?"

She looked as though I had paid her a compliment. "Of course," she said, smiling widely. "He was a pig of a man with a terrible temper. It was unbearable being married to him, so when I took out the life insurance policy, I figured it needed to be for a long time, so suspicion wouldn't fall on me."

One thing had puzzled me. "But why did you put the vial of Botox in the waiter's pocket?" I asked her. "Were you trying to frame him?"

Her expression darkened. "No! I'm not that stupid! It was so the police would know Marcus was poisoned with Botox."

"But how did that help you?" I asked, genuinely puzzled.

She waved the gun a little and I broke into a cold sweat. "I didn't want the medical examiner to take too long trying to figure out what happened to Marcus. I wanted them to know he was poisoned, and with Botox as soon as possible. That way the medical examiner would sign off on his body and the insurance claim could be processed even faster."

"Are insurance claims paid out on murder victims?" I asked her.

She looked surprised. "Yes, they are! Just not to the murderer, obviously, which is exactly why I planned it for ten years. I've already lodged a claim. And just in the nick of time too, because Marcus ran the business into the ground. I made sure the businesses were only in his name," she said, "so I'm not responsible for any of his debts."

"Were you trying to frame anyone for the murder?" I asked her.

"No," she said. "In crime, it's better to keep it simple. I just didn't want the police to suspect me. I only invented the story about Marcus blackmailing

Ted because the police were getting too close. I've played the part of a loving wife for decades now, so when the police asked around, everyone would say we never quarreled. And of course we didn't quarrel, because I put on a good act. I was biding my time and now I'll have plenty of money and none of his debts. It was worth the wait."

I thought she was quite unbalanced. "But how did you discover Candace was suspicious of you?"

"It was that idiot Cherri," she said. "She told me she suspected Candace and Rick as they were friends with Dr. Davidson. I told her a private investigator had come to see me. She told me she had hired the private investigator and that the woman was your roommate. I was at Candace's house earlier and I told her Cherri had hired a private investigator. We got to talking, and then Candace brought up something that happened when I was in junior high. My best friend stole my boyfriend from me. I was devastated, so I got her back."

"You took revenge ten years later," I said.

She nodded. "I told you, I'm a patient woman. I waited until she married, and then I had an affair with her husband who happened to be a private investigator. That's why the subject came up, you see. I could tell Candace was suspicious. I pretended to leave Candace's house, but parked my car out back. I sneaked back into the house and heard her speaking with you on the phone."

"And that's when you hit her with the candlestick?" I said.

She nodded. "And I hid in another room and waited for you to come so I could finish you off too. I wanted to make it look like the two of you had a struggle, only when you got here, you didn't seem to know anything and Candace had lost her memory."

"But why didn't you kill her?" I asked her.

"I thought I did," she said. "That woman is tough. I hit her really hard and she went out cold, so I thought she was dead."

"Where did you get the Botox?"

"I stole it from the nurse at Candace's Botox parties."

She advanced toward me, a menacing look on her face. As she raised her gun, she almost tripped over Mr. Crumbles. She aimed a kick at him, but he was too fast for her.

I shut my eyes tightly, waiting for the inevitable. So this was how it was going to end. Everything seemed to stand still.

I heard a gunshot but felt no pain. I opened my eyes.

Melissa was lying face down on the ground trying to catch her breath. Mr. Crumbles was sitting on her back, looking pleased with himself. The gun was lying near her hand, so I wasted no time picking it up.

It took me a moment to realize what had happened. In my hurry over Candace's call, I had not moved the cat activity tree from its position adjacent to the pole. Mr. Crumbles had climbed on the top of the pole and had done what he usually did—swinging down and letting go, the momentum flinging him across the room. Melissa had been standing too close and he had hit her hard, right in the small of the back, and had winded her.

I aimed the gun at her with one hand, and then called Detective McCloud with the other.

CHAPTER 20

The following morning, I was at the pond on my sister's farm. Rebecca had insisted we take the morning off to have a picnic. She said nothing was more important than family, and she was concerned about my close call.

Matilda, Eleanor, Rebecca, and I were laughing at the antics of the ducklings. It was a beautiful sunny day, with a gentle breeze forming little ripples on the pond. I sighed with relief that everything had turned out all right.

Candace was recovering nicely and her husband, Rick, had called to thank me. Cherri and Ted had gone back to New York. I can't say I was sorry, although I did feel a little sorry for Cherri.

Ted had sent along a curt note to say I had to sign the papers and return them to him in one week. The papers were about the family trust. I had thought that was covered in the prenup, but maybe not, given that Ted was so keen for me to sign. Maybe my lawyer would have some good news for me, and I had no intention of meeting Ted's one-week deadline.

"All things work together for good to those who love God," Rebecca quoted, and I shook my finger at her.

"As you well know, I was Amish once and I know that you'd be in trouble for showing off the fact you can recite Scripture. You're lucky none of us here are Amish."

Rebecca chuckled. "It wouldn't be the first time I've been called *Scripture Smart*."

"Jane, have you had a chance to look at the papers Ted wanted you to sign?" Eleanor asked me.

"I'd completely forgotten about them!" I exclaimed. "Never mind, I'll make an appointment with my lawyer this week."

"Is it time to eat?" Matilda said, rubbing her rumbling stomach. Now that I thought about it, I was hungry too.

Rebecca made to move, but I waved her back down.

"You're supposed to be taking it easy and yet you've brought food," I admonished her.

Rebecca opened her picnic basket to reveal a Shoo-fly pie, an apple pie, as well as fried chicken, peppered deviled eggs, and cornbread salad. "The ladies have been bringing me lots of food," she said with a smile.

"I made some whoopie pies," I told her. "I brought the chocolate beet cake as well. We haven't had a chance to eat it yet." I opened my basket to reveal whoopie pies in various flavors: chocolate, strawberry, vanilla, peanut butter, pumpkin, oatmeal, and maple.

Matilda looked up from spreading a picnic blanket in front of us. "We'll certainly eat well today."

I watched Rebecca's buggy horse grazing alongside Ephraim's buggy horse in the field on the other side of the pond. They were grazing contentedly, occasionally swishing their tails against an offending fly.

"I can't believe that cat saved you again," Rebecca said. "I baked him some chicken treats as a reward. Don't let me forget to give them to you, Eleanor."

Eleanor thanked her. "I'll pop back to the car and fetch my picnic basket," she said. "I did a lot of baking last night for the picnic. I even attempted a funeral pie."

Matilda gasped. "Honestly, Eleanor! How could you make a *funeral* pie after Jane had such a close call?"

Rebecca and I laughed. Eleanor shot Matilda a look before hurrying to the car. She presently returned, struggling under the weight of the picnic basket.

"You did do a lot of baking," Rebecca said.

She nodded. "Yes, I hope you like it." The three of us leaned over the basket to see what goodies Eleanor had baked.

She lifted off the lid. We all gasped.

There, lying in the picnic basket fast asleep, was none other than Mr. Crumbles.

"How did he get in there?" I said.

"He ate most of the cakes!" Matilda exclaimed. "And he's squashed that sponge cake flat!"

Rebecca just sat there, her jaw wide open.

"What are we going to do with him while we have the picnic?" Matilda said.

"He can sleep on the grass," Eleanor said. "He's too full and sleepy to run away. Naughty Mr. Crumbles." However, she said it in such a gentle tone I don't think Mr. Crumbles would have minded, even if he had been awake.

Eleanor picked him up and deposited him on the grass beside us. He barely moved. "He's sleeping well because he's eaten too much," Matilda said.

"Mr. Crumbles can do whatever he likes as far as I'm concerned," I said. "I'll even get him another pole if he wants one." I took one look at Rebecca's face and then quickly added, "That was a joke. Anyway, I'm going to buy him a lifetime supply of treats."

Mr. Crumbles opened one eye briefly but other than that, did not move a muscle.

Soon all of us, with the exception of Mr. Crumbles who was still fast asleep, were relaxing on the soft grass, drinking homemade lemonade and eating a veritable feast.

"This is lovely," I said. "Thanks for suggesting it, Rebecca."

"I'm just glad you're all right," she said.

All of a sudden I heard a car and craned my neck to see who it was. To my surprise, it was

Damon. I instinctively smoothed down my hair as he strolled toward us.

I muttered to the others, "It's Detective McCloud. I wonder what he's doing here? I hope no one else has been murdered." My heart fluttered.

Matilda and Eleanor laughed as if I had said something funny.

As he approached, he nodded to Matilda and she nodded back. Hmm, so Matilda had told him we were there.

"I was just passing by when I saw your car, Jane," he said, smiling. I'm sure he didn't expect me to believe it.

"It's good to see you," I said shyly. "Would you like to share our picnic?"

"I'd love to, but I'm on duty today, more's the pity."

I could see Rebecca frowning. I figured she was trying to make out his words. I didn't need to strain to understand him. By now I was growing accustomed to his Scottish accent.

"You look much happier than you looked last night," he said. Damon and Detective Stirling had come to arrest Melissa, and Damon had stayed back to take my witness statement.

"You're probably tired of taking witness statements from me," I said with a laugh.

Damon looked as though he was about to say something but hesitated. "Yes, you're always getting yourself into trouble. There's nothing I can do about that, but at least I can make sure you stay dry." With that, he handed me an umbrella.

It wasn't a standard dark umbrella. Rather, it was yellow and black with a thin red stripe.

"An umbrella? For me?" I said, my cheeks burning.

"Yes, as you obviously don't have one," Damon said. "It's the McCloud tartan, and it has your name on it, so there won't be any danger of it getting stolen."

"Thank you, thank you so much," I stammered.

"Are you sure you couldn't stay for a piece of chocolate beet cake?" Matilda pressed him. "Jane made it."

"If you put it like that," he said with a smile. He sat next to me, so close our shoulders were almost touching.

The five of us sat in companionable silence, enjoying the meal, and looking out over the beautiful pond and the grass gently blowing in the breeze.

I had left my old life behind. I had been through an ordeal and had come out the other side happier than ever. I reflected that while storms will invariably come, they always do pass and are replaced by sunshine, and there's always a rainbow on the other side.

AMISH RECIPE

AMISH FUNERAL PIE

INGREDIENTS

    2 cups raisins
    2 cups water
    finely grated zest of 1 large orange
    1 cup orange juice
    1/2 cup brown sugar
    1/2 cup granulated sugar
    1 tablespoon granulated sugar
    2 tablespoons cornstarch
    3/4 teaspoon ground allspice
    1/4 teaspoon freshly grated nutmeg
    1 1/4 teaspoons ground cinnamon
    1 tablespoon lemon juice
    1/2 cup chopped walnuts
    1 egg, beaten

3 tablespoons butter

METHOD

Preheat oven to 425 degrees F.

Combine raisins, water, orange zest and juice in a saucepan. Bring to a boil. Reduce heat and simmer for 5 minutes.

Combine 3/4 cup granulated sugar, cornstarch, allspice, cinnamon, and nutmeg in a small bowl.

Stir slowly into raisin mixture. Cook, stirring constantly, until thickened, about 2 minutes. Remove pan from heat. Stir in lemon juice and walnuts.

PASTRY

INGREDIENTS

3 cups all purpose flour

1 teaspoon salt

1 cup Crisco or butter

1 large egg

1/3 cup cold water

1 tablespoon apple cider vinegar

Combine the flour and salt.

METHOD

Add the Crisco or butter. Rub in.

Add egg, water, and apple cider vinegar.

Roll out half the dough to a 1/8-inch thickness onto a floured surface.

Fit the dough into a 9 inch pie pan.

Pour filling into pie shell.

Trim the edges to an overhang. Seal edges and crimp the edges with a fork.

Roll out remaining pastry and place over pie. Seal edges.

Cut several slashes into top of pie. Brush with beaten egg and sprinkle sugar on top.

Bake until golden, 20 - 25 minutes.

AMISH RECIPE

AMISH RED BEET CHOCOLATE CAKE

INGREDIENTS

    1 1/2 cups all purpose flour

    1/4 cup dutch cocoa powder

    3/4 cup vegetable oil

    1 1/4 cup brown sugar

    1/2 cup maple syrup

    1 cup dark chocolate chips

    1 1/2 cups beet, cooked and pureed

    3 eggs, lightly beaten

    1/2 teaspoon salt

    1/2 teaspoon baking soda

    1 teaspoon vanilla extract

GANACHE

    3/4 cup thin cream

    1 cup dark chocolate chips

1 tablespoon maple syrup

METHOD

Cover beets with water in a pot. Bring to the boil. Reduce heat. Simmer 30 minutes until tender. Drain and puree until smooth.

Coat a 9 inch diameter cake pan. Preheat oven to 350°F.

Mix together the flour, baking soda, and salt.

Combine sugar, beaten eggs, and oil in a large bowl. Stir well.

Blend in the pureed beets, melted chocolate, and vanilla.

Gradually add the dry ingredients to the beet mixture, beating well.

Pour into the prepared pan. Bake 40 to 45 minutes.

Cool in the pan. Cover and let stand overnight.

GANACHE

Combine thin cream, chocolate chips, and maple syrup in a small saucepan over low heat. Stir over a low to medium heat for 5 minutes or until mixture is glossy. Make sure chocolate is melted.

Leave to cool until the mixture thickens slightly (5-10 minutes). Pour over the cake.

NEXT BOOK IN THIS SERIES

AN AMISH CUPCAKE COZY MYSTERY -
BOOK 3

Confection is Good for the Soul

Judy Jenkins, part-time cupcake book author and full-time bully, is dead . . . but why do the police suspect Jane's sweet Amish sister, Rebecca?

When Rebecca is accused of murder -- all over Amish Sour Cream Spice cupcakes -- it's the start of another thrilling mystery for Jane Delight.

Jane is eager to clear Rebecca's name, but with brooding Detective Damon McCloud wanting to whisk her away from the suspects, she's in for the adventure of a lifetime.

Can Jane, Mr. Crumbles the cat, and Jane's

meddlesome octogenarian roommates, Matilda and Eleanor, cook up a plan to save the day?

Or is this mystery going to end in heart-bake?

ABOUT RUTH HARTZLER

USA Today Bestselling author Ruth Hartzler spends her days writing, walking her dog, and thinking of ways to murder somebody. That's because Ruth writes cozy mysteries and thrillers.

She is best known for her archaeological adventures, for which she relies upon her former career as a college professor of ancient languages and Biblical history.

www.ruthhartzler.com